Blood of Their Sons

This book is a work of fiction.
It is intended for adult readers. It contains
language some may consider obscene.

Cover Design: Sherrye Alves
salves47@yahoo.com

ISBN: 978-0-982954515

Frog's Hair Press
PO Box 34483
Charlotte, NC 28234

www.frogshairpress.com

frogshairpress@gmail.com

Printed in the United States.

Second Edition

Acknowledgment

~ *Q*~

This story gives a small glimpse of my growing up and some of the cultural events that flavored my life. In that regard, I am thankful for my family and the creativity they inspired.

To the southern reader: may you see a speck of your mother or grandmother, aunt or brother, neighbor or friend somewhere in these pages.

Please enjoy...

~ SUKU ~

Special Thanks

As you read, you will come across chapter headings with the word SuKu. SuKu is an ascendant from the realm of Spirit who agreed to help me tell this story. There were things I could not know, so cannot tell. In her realm, Beings are objects no greater than *The* Trees, *The* Birds, *The* Wind. They are objects in the tapestry of Creation; she speaks of them as such. My gratitude to her is endless.

Grace St.John

"In all thy getting, get understanding."

(Proverbs 4:7 KJV)

Blood of Their Sons

Chapter 2: *Loss*

I resented my mother. It wasn't obvious to others, but I'm sure she knew. The counselor I chose was not gifted to the degree as I, but clearly had insight. I had gone on about my mother leaving me when she asks, out of nowhere, "Tell me about your son."

"What?"

"The child you lost. Tell me about him."

"There's nothing to tell."

"Then why are you angry?"

"Because my mother took something from me!"

"Your child?"

"No, my child 'hood'."

"So, your anger is about loss?"

"My anger is about abandonment."

"Do you think you abandoned your child, Grace, the one you lost?"

"How could I have saved him? It was a miscarriage. I was perfectly healthy, did everything right, but he died anyway. Inside my body. There was no one to blame."

"And yet, you do."

Chapter 3: *Going Home*

No one talked about why my mother left us, what kept Aunt Olivia away for thirty years and why my brother, Dillon, a vibrant young man, was dead. No one spoke ever about being the first-born female of the first-born female of generations of first-born women. I spoke into the abyss for answers. A voice in my head said, *Go home.*

Thoughts of growing up— some good, some not— kept me company on the drive. Traffic was heavy for a Saturday morning. An accident forced cars to move like inchworms on Valium. Heat had already begun to crawl into my skin and stay.

To deny the thoughts I knew would come I pressed numbers into the cell phone. I could almost hear the signal roam from a local satellite and bounce to Shannon's home phone. She answered on the second ring.

"Hi baby, what's up?"

"Hey mom! Where are you?"

"Stuck in traffic. Calling you from this brick they call a wireless phone. Planned to see Mama and Granny today but if this backup doesn't move before I get to the next exit, I'm headed back home. My lungs are sizzling."

"So, what's up?"

"Two things. First, how's my grandson?"

"Wren is great. He's kicking as we speak."

2

"Aw.. he knows his Gaia's calling."

"You are definitely an earth goddess, but you're gonna be 'Grandma,' like everybody else. What's the second thing?"

"Come to Blessing today. I had one of my inclinations. This one said, 'get Shannon to Nola's house.'" We both laughed. "It's probably because I haven't seen my only child in weeks. My baby is having a baby and I don't want to miss a minute. Come visit with me. Let me look at you."

I sensed Shannon's laugh fade to a smile. Although cloaked in humor, she knew to take my 'inclination' seriously. Shannon was a first-born, and would soon give birth to the next generation, albeit, breaking the gender heritage. When we learned it was a boy, I felt an odd sense of grief. Shannon had held my hand and laid her head on my shoulder and apologized as if she had done something wrong.

I interrupted her silence. "Knowing I'll see you today will make being stuck in this heat bearable. What say you, my precious baby girl?"

"Okay, mom. I'll meet you there."

I hung up and held the phone next to my cheek. When we came home from the hospital, and were alone for the first time, I had held her in my arms, close to my face. For a child just days old, she was exceptionally alert. I folded back the blanket and caressed her hair. Already two inches long at birth, the thick lockets were like a shining aurora circling her head. I brushed her cheeks with my finger and peered into knowing eyes that stared back. My eyes glistened and I couldn't help but smile from way down deep. Shannon smiled, too. As if trying to speak, she moved her lips and a bubble grew. I covered my little girl's face with mine and washed her with my tears. Warmth burned in my heart like nothing I'd ever felt. Not before, not since. Not like that moment.

Without notice, the memory I had forced at bay found a crack in my resistance. What happened that night, on the dark side of the moon, had become graffiti on my soul. Some days I stared at it. Today, it stared at me.

Yes, I had to go home— to face Nola, to confront Grandmother. These women were linked to the fear growing in me; they would know its name. Sadly, I would learn the price of being the first-born female of the first-born female of generations of first-born women who bore the name, St.John.

Chapter 4: *SuKu - MaeAlice*

I am SuKu, Spirit from the realm of Awareness, ascendant of the St.John clan, descendant to the Others before me. We are Seen and Unseen, Known and Unknown.

For most of The MaeAlice's years, life was a narrow strip of smoldering ash, sprinkled with shards of glass, and she walked it barefoot. Perhaps it was being born black, and a woman at a time when neither was valued. Every now and then, an ash had cooled or a patch of glass worn harmless by those who had gone before.

Much of her burden was blamed on the grandchildren dumped on her to keep. That's how she saw it. They were only to be there a little while. A little while turned into years. Along with anyone who listened, they knew their part in her misery.

The stroke didn't disfigure her; her mouth didn't contort, her arms didn't withdraw. But something did change in her countenance. It was odd; everyone said she became beautiful. She had the look of moonlit water. The stroke took her mind but gave her gentleness. Some thought it gave a better trade than what it took.

The word went out. Anyone wanting to pay respects should come. Church matrons sat in folding chairs around the metal bed built for one, and pretended to pray. Behind her back they asked each other, "Who does she think she is," rebuking anything MaeAlice dared to do, this woman who dared often. She did not want them at her side. But The MaeAlice was one of them, a member of this unrehearsed troupe, performing this unwritten act. She pretended to appreciate their presence; they pretended to care.

"Lord, Miss Mae, you blessed to see another day. The Lord's gon' take care of you," they'd say. "You get your strength back. We-alls praying for you. Girl, the usher board just ain't the same. You get yourself better, you hear."

Next to gardening, chopping wood was her favorite thing to do. A time came when she enjoyed burning wood just as much. Year round, heat formed a wavy gauntlet through which anyone wanting a peek into her sanctum had to pass. Not many made the sojourn. But there she could be found, sitting two feet from the flames, rocking to a rhythm only she knew. She was queen and the flickers her servants. Sometimes it seemed fire was the master, and she its loyal subject. Keeping the fire alive was why she chopped wood—to feed the red belly of her savior. The cast iron beast sat in her bedroom like a forsaken Buddha. It warmed her flesh and warded off all others.

Now, here she lay, gripping the bars of a tiny metal bed in another room cloaked in heat. Her visitors rocked their overweight bodies and moaned a song that didn't resemble any gospel heard on Sunday. The sound came off their tongues and fell like broken glass.

The scowl MaeAlice had perfected early in life twisted across her face. Flesh stretched tight across her cheeks and hung like muffs below her ears. The legs every woman envied for years now sagged like too much cloth in a pair of slacks. They looked like a little boy wearing his father's britches.

She'd all but stopped digesting more than a spoonful of anything. Bits of what she did eat could be found in the folds of her bedspread, or her skin. She confused the two sometimes. Had she not been darker than the floral brown covers, it would have been difficult to tell one fold from another.

The MaeAlice and Grace shared something that had no name. It guided her back. She was the keeper of MaeAlice's secrets, and she had one more to tell.

Chapter 5: *Hog Killing*

It was October when Olivia left. I was almost ten. This time of year was important to our survival. Along with gifts of fruits and vegetables Grandmother preserved from the earth, a pig was the staple meat to get us through the winter. One was selected a few months before and put into a small stall made of reject pieces from Mr. Jim's lumberyard. He often gave Grandmother these remnants of his guilt.

There was no man in Grandmother's house. Not now, anyway. Ted had been gone for two weeks. Everyone suspected he would not be coming back. Knowing that, some of the men around the neighborhood came to help with the killing. Most were glad he was gone. Even if Ted were around, he'd be little use in hog killing. He was a city boy. The men who came would have come anyway. They'd work the whole day for a jar of the corn liquor illegally made in the woods behind a barn, and illegally sold in Grandmother's kitchen. The brew master, an old Indian man, was nice, though he didn't look it. He had no teeth and his hair hung in strings across his face. Everyone said his moonshine had to be stolen from God. Others teased it was flavored by the drippings from his hair.

Three men helped to kill hog that day. They stood around laughing over some exaggerated story until Grandmother was ready. Hog killing was a daylong chore that turned into a weekend event. Two of the men didn't have jobs so there was no boss to lie to about not coming in today. One had a job he didn't want and hoped he wouldn't have come Monday. He'd never quit even though he hated the trade that paid him fifty dollars less each week than he needed to make ends meet.

A hole had been dug in the ground earlier that morning and piled with wood and kindling. To us children, kindling was magic. It didn't take much to bring a fire to two-foot flames. Grandmother did her favorite thing while the hole was being dug: she split wood. One of the men laughed out. "Tonight, Eva Lee's legs gon' split just like that." His partners laughed in agreement.

7

The third man tended the fire. Everyone did as this man instructed. Except Grandmother. Out of earshot, the other men talked about the man who took orders from her. "He's got some kind of power," one said. "Watch him, he's gon' talk to that pig. They say he talks something out the animal's body so when the pig dies, the meat won't go bad." No one ever said what the something was. The first man didn't know how he did it but swore it was true.

"I seen him do it," one man exclaimed. "That pig must have knowed he was about to die cause he starts wailing and running around in that stall. The other ones huddle in a corner and squeal like babies. The man walks to the pen. He stands there, looking at that pig like he was reading his mind, never said a word. The pig stopped wailing and stomping. All he did was grunt one time, then nothing."

The second man held onto every word. So did I. The storyteller slowed the telling. He lowered his voice and spoke the next sentence with effect.

"The pig turns to face the man and don't move. The man reaches inside that heavy leather coat he wears and pulls out a gun. It's a rifle with a barrel as long as my leg. Without taking his eyes off that pig, he raises the rifle and aims it 'bout four feet from the pig's head. Pig stands still. Then, BAM! One shot between the eyes with the pig look-ing straight at him."

The storyteller stopped telling. He looked each listener in the eye to show how the pig looked at the man. Wide-eyed, he spoke his last sentence. "The pig drops to his knees. Dead"

I stared at the third man. He never said much, even when he told us what to bring from the kitchen. He would say "Pot," and we scrambled to bring one back. He looked at it and nodded that one would do.

8

The man was old. Like with Grandmother, no one knew his age with any degree of certainty. Some said he came on the first ship from Africa. His skin was as worn as his coat, but had a beautiful glow. Balls of hair more silver than black sat all over his head like tiny boles of cotton. A vein on the side of his temple lay like a sun-dried worm. He never opened them much so his eyes looked like a crooked river that went nowhere. A scruffy mustache and matted beard, the same color as his hair, moved up and down with each chew on whatever was wadded in his cheek. He put on his coat. Three snaps remained on the tattered leather that had a dozen hooks.

The hog killer dipped his hands into the wash pot, cupped out a handful of water and rubbed it around like a doctor preparing for surgery. Steam rose from the small bubbles that had formed on the surface. He seemed not to notice. Sure enough, just as the storyteller said, the pigs began to squeal as soon as the third man approached them. He walked over to the special pig and stared at its back. Its hooves paced the wooden floor in one spot in a corner of the stall. The man stood still. Soon, the pig stopped scuffling and turned around. His snout was to the floor and he snorted hard, tired from his failed escape. The man's hands hung loosely by his side. Water dripped from his dark, knotty fingers.

Everyone stood still, saying nothing, watching the figure who looked like the bad man in a western movie. Eventually, the pig looked up from the floor. When he did, the man folded open his leather coat and pulled out a rifle. He raised the sight on the long barrel to his eye, his movements choreographed. He waited. The pig lowered his head, blinked and looked up again. Everything was still. A sharp whistle pierced the silence. The pig's front knees buckled, and then he fell. The man turned, and walked a few quiet steps, another movement in his dance.

The other men hoisted the pig onto a tall workhorse they'd erected a few days ago. His head swung slightly like a pendulum over the hole beneath his snout. The wash pot boiled nearby.

The hog-killer put the Winchester back into his coat. In the same motion, his hand returned with a machete. Grim faces were carved in the wood of the mahogany handle. Age encrusted the blade black and brown, except for the thin streak of silver that glimmered the whole length of its two-foot shaft. The old man's arm moved outward like a geisha. This frightening thing caught the morning sun. The man walked up to the dead pig. He mumbled something and raised his knife. Grandmother caught his hand. She took the knife from him and with one swift motion, cut the pig's throat from left to right, backhanded. Blood squirted onto her matted sweater and splattered her face. The rest gushed from the pig's body and poured in a heavy stream into the hole beneath him. Grandmother wiped the blood from her face with the back of her hand. I thought I saw a small stumble as she backed away.

Chapter 6: *The Lesson*

The hog killing was done.

The third man took his plate and sat on the ground underneath the white willow tree that shaded the back of the house. He propped his knees to his chest. I wadded a paper towel around my pork rinds and sat on the ground near him. I chewed and swallowed and watched. The old man said nothing for the longest time.

Finally, he spoke. "You are a special child. Like yor gran'mudda, but dif-fer-ent. You know dis, yes?" he asked. "You see beyond da living. You hear beyond the word. Yes?" He spoke— not so much asking as telling. "What you want to know little one."

I was surprised that he did not humor me, that he knew I had questions. Without his offer, I would never have asked. "I want to know what you did to the pig."

"I did no-thing to the pig. What you must unda'stand, little one, is all things have purpose. God requires all things to be revered. And yet everything is to serve. Some things are here solely so that other things may live. You understand dis?"

He looked at me for a long time. I finally nodded yes. Even through the heavy African dialect--from where and how long ago, I did not know; it didn't matter--I understood him.

He added, "No life is ever lost, little one. Death is a mere step along the sacred journey. This you will know in time."

The other two men stayed to help Grandmother finish up. They were sufficiently fed and on the road to drunk. I found a spot close by to chew on the pork skins I had left. The men had become accustomed to me being around all day so didn't hold back as they resumed telling stories. They were still sober enough to pour from the Mason jar into the jelly glasses Grandmother had set on the table.

Dusk had begun to drape the evening. The man who had a job talked about his hatred for it. They shared each other's misery on that subject for some time.

"It was a good day for killing," one said. The other agreed. Another discourse followed about someone who had been caught by the police and almost beaten to death. "Po thang," he offered, speaking about the mother. "She already got one boy in prison. Look like this one going there, too."

Not caring for that subject, for its stark reality over which they could do nothing, the other man said something about Eva Lee's legs parting, a subject each relished, and had intimate knowledge.

"I'm gon' git some of that tonight," the man with a job said.

"Pay for a round for me, while you're in there," the other coaxed.

"You may as well hump that hole in the ground when I'm finish with her," the job man teased.

They laughed. Talk of Eva Lee's legs led them to Grandmother. Their recognition held as much appreciation for the woman as for her legs. No woman could challenge Grandmother in that contest.

"She handles that ax better than any man I know," the jobless man offered.

"I'd hate to cross her with that thing nearby. You could lose a leg and never know it till you took a step to run."

A few more opinions led them to Ted. "He ain't likely to show up around here again."

"Nope, not in one piece anyway, not after what he done."

"How could he do that to Mae? What kind of man would do that?"

They both turned up the jelly glass they cupped in both hands, quickly found their mouths, and swallowed deep.

12

Ted had been Grandmother's lover. One of the pig killers said he was 'slick as snail snot and smooth as fresh-made butter.' They all laughed. They appreciated Ted's good looks and style but could not say so directly.

"If I had just a taste of what he's got, man, shoot. All the women this side of town would be mine."

"Yeah, and the other side would be mine." A roar of laughter, and coughs and slapping of knees followed.

Hearing the men talk reminded me of the first day I saw Ted. He was far younger than Grandmother. He had come from Baltimore and was the guest of one of her customers. Along with beer and moonshine, she served up bottles of cheap gin and vodka purchased at the ABC store and sold at a premium. Most everyone started with a beer or fifty cent shot and worked their way up to dollar drinks when they were bold enough, or drunk enough not to care about the groceries the money was meant to buy.

Grandmother wore an apron with deep pockets when she served drinks; she never wore one to cook. This one, like the garden apron that held the seeds and fertilizer for her labor, contained the elements of her trade— a towel for drying glasses, quarters to make change. One pocket held bills. Like the bounty of her garden, business was always good.

Grandmother never learned to read and write, but she could count. Even better, her memory was precise. She knew exactly how many drinks each person had had, and at what price calculated to the drop. Before they got too drunk or pretended to, she settled their debt. Every now and then one had enough sheets in the wind to challenge her on the bill or try not paying at all. Once, a newcomer thought he'd show off to his friend. "I ain't giving her shit.

Her goddamn liquor watered down anyway." The words drooled from his lips on a strand of spit.

Grandmother left the room. Others tried to warn the fool of his mistake. But this one had to test MaeAlice's manhood. When she returned, the fool was saying, "If she mess with me, I'll call the po..." Before he could get out "...leese," she had raised her ax with the flat side facing his head. He never finished his sentence. Those who had warned him stepped back, outside the scope of her swing.

Someone yelled. "No, Miss Mae, don't!" and grabbed the handle midair.

Scared sober, the man jerked one hand up to protect his head while the other scrambled to his pocket to find the five dollars he owed. A trembling hand reached it to her.

"I don't want nothing from your hands. Put it on the table, there," she commanded. When he obeyed, she looked at his two companions and told them, "Get this bastard out of my house and never bring him back."

One was a regular who lived about three miles away. The other newcomer was Ted.

Chapter 7: *The Return*

I made my way to the back bedroom where Grandmother lay dying. An oversized television sat atop a dresser like a billboard. The cataracts and glaucoma veiled her once brown eyes with a gray film that refused her visual participation in this world with any degree of clarity. I found her fetal-like, turned away. Grandmother was bundled in a cotton smock she had tried to remove. The top of it lay open enough to expose the side of a withered breast. The

bed covers lay in disarray. One of the beautiful legs everyone revered lay on top of the bedspread like an excavated
bone.

Softly, I called, "Hi, Granny."

She turned her face from the pillow. Her eyelids flut-
tered and began to separate.

"It's me, Grace."

A smile came to a pair of toothless lips. In the voice she
reserved for those she favored, she recited the nursery
rhyme she'd sing when she wanted to show me love.
"Monday's child is fair of face, Tuesday's child is full of
grace...." I was born on Tuesday. Grace became a nick-
name. I could have been born a Wednesday's child who is
full of woe, or Thursday's child who has far to go. Poor
Saturday's child works hard for a living. Yes, I could have
been born on any of those days. So could the woman who
lay before me.

"When you get here," she asked, still singing her
words.

"A few minutes ago." I pulled at the thin bedspread to
cover her skeleton. "Are you thirsty; you hungry? Mama
made mashed potatoes, chicken and stewed okra. All your
favorites. I'll get you some and you can tell me what Victor
is doing on 'The Young and the Restless'."

"Okay." The word was sweet, like an old man tempt-
ing a young girl with candy. Grandmother's voice had not
lost its power like the rest of her. But this voice was reserved for me.

I had been Grandmother's confidante and personal sec-
retary until I left for college. I read letters to her and wrote
back to the senders. I knew whose husband beat her,
whose son got locked up, whose daughter got pregnant.
Who died that Grandmother didn't remember or sometime

said good riddance. Who graduated from high school and what job someone had that made them think more of themselves than they should. Equally, I knew Grandmother's response— both the one she sent in reply and the ones I couldn't put on paper.

A surge of pity burned in my throat to see her this way. Grandmother had resigned to using her gums long ago after her store bought teeth went missing. Before that, she kept them in water on her dresser to scare little children into obedience. Most likely, one of them was the reason her teeth were gone.

The doctors said she had tumors in her esophagus and stomach. These tumors, that had no name, caused her considerable pain. Nola would never admit they were cancer. Whatever they were, the polyps were the reason Grandmother had stopped eating. Medication helped, but not enough.

"Shannon is coming to join us, Granny. You should see how big she's gotten. We thought she might have twins until the doctor said it was just a big baby."

"She's gon' have a beautiful baby girl," Grandmother said.

"It's a boy," I beamed. "Shannon is going to break the first-born female trend." It was a secret Shannon and I agreed to keep, but I couldn't help myself.

"No, no; she can't" Grandmother answered.

Her agitation startled me, so I changed the subject. We made small talk about nothing in particular between clicks and swallows. Mostly, we sat quietly in each other's company. Voices came from the television looming atop the dresser but they didn't have her attention. Her eyes focused on the seat at the foot of her bed. She turned to me and said, "Do you see him, Grace? Do you see him?"

I turned my head to the place of her attention. "Yes, Granny, I see him."

Chapter 8: *Discovery*

I learned an important fact about myself when I was nine. It was my first awakening of what it meant to be the first-born female of the first-born female of the first-born female of unknown generations before Grandmother's mother. We saw, felt, and knew things others did not.

I spent a lot of time in the cemetery back then. It was my favorite place to get away to my thoughts. No one came to there. Fear of the dead. If they needed me, they'd call, yelling my name if I took too long coming.

I had not seen the woman come into the cemetery. Was surprised when I looked up from my book and saw her several rows away. She wore a black fur coat even though it was summer. A short ruffled veil spewed from the top of her hat like a flower too heavy for the stem. I followed the woman with my eyes, thinking she must be looking for someone, a family member to visit. The visitor moved slowly through the rows, came to a new tombstone, stopped and knelt. I could no longer see her but continued to watch.

After several minutes, when she hadn't stood up, I called out, "Miss, are you all right?" No answer. I walked to where I thought she'd gone. The etching on the stone where she'd stopped read: 'Shelia Paxon. Loving Wife. Gone Home.' I looked around but the woman was nowhere in sight. Looking again at the dates on the tombstone, I thought it odd; I didn't remember anyone being buried recently. It could have happened while I was in school. That made it doubly odd since most funerals took place on the weekend. No one could afford to have a day taken from a paycheck that was already too short. After another glance around, I went back to my book.

My material gift developed in my teens. I came to know things instinctively. Without looking at a clock, I always knew the time within five minutes of my guess. Grandmother's customers made me their timekeeper, especially the men who had to get home before their wives started calling, or worse, came looking. They paid me a quarter for my services. I've never worn a watch— not even now.

Better than that, I could sense people's character. I knew things about them I had no reason to know. It was as if I pulled the answer out of air. With this gift, I earned my living. That ability only failed me once.

Chapter 9: *Acknowledgment*

Grandmother exhaled the small breath in her lungs. "Do you remember the old man who use to kill hogs for me?"

"I do. In fact, I thought about him today."

Grandmother continued without recognizing the coincidence. "He looked at you one day with that look in his eyes. I knew what he saw. He had it, too. Did he tell you?"

I smiled at grandmother and shook my head yes. It was the first time she had ever acknowledged my gift, or her own. I wondered what else she knew; but it was time to listen.

"He was a powerful man," she said. "Some say he was a hundred years old. Some say he never aged. Could be both is true." Grandmother looked at me. "You the only one I can count on, Grace. You always was the only one I could trust."

Grandmother gripped my hand. She was strong to look so frail. Her head turned sharply from the TV to gaze at the end of her bed. She trembled. "I had to," she said, looking at the visitor. "He comes and stands there, looking at me. He don't talk. He just looks at me. I close my eyes and try to sleep, hoping he'll be gone. But he don't leave. I holler for Nola but she can't see him; tells me ain't nobody there."

I looked to the end of the bed, following grandmother's eyes, my hands still locked around her own. I was probably squeezing too tightly but I didn't know what else to do. Grandmother lay still, her breathing irregular and slow, her eyelids stuck to one another. It was as if she had left her body and expected me to hold onto her in case she lost her way.

The stroke had returned her to the events that put this sad moment in motion. It was one hour, one night that changed every life around her, and followed us across time.

Ted was at the foot of grandmother's bed. I saw him there every visit. He never spoke; I never acknowledged him. Today I would have to because she saw him, too. "Don't worry; he can't hurt you," I told her.

Seeing him took me to the first day we met. This is how he chose to appear, as he did that day. Ted was good looking by anyone's standard, and he knew it. Every woman in Blessing said he was fine as frog's hair. When he first arrived at Grandmother's house those years ago, I thought he must be famous. No one in my world looked like Ted.

I was propped against the white willow tree engrossed in my favorite past time when he arrived that day, the same day as the woman in the cemetery. Ted stooped and asked about the book I was reading. He read the title out loud, '*The Keepers of Carifa.*' "Sounds interesting," he said. I was shy and only nodded on cue in our one-sided conversation. Finally, he asked where he could find the lady of the house. I lifted my nine-year-old finger and pointed.

I watched his slow stride to the backyard where Grandmother chopped weeds from the garden. I'd seen enough of Grandmother's customers to tell them apart: the ones who were confident and the ones who were afraid. Ted had no fear. As I watched him glide towards the backyard, I glanced the ground behind him. I blinked and rubbed my eyes. Maybe I'd been reading too long. I squinted in his direction. It was still there, another shadow just slightly to the right of his own, almost indiscernible but there. I stood up and looked for my own thin, elongated shadow. Turned so it was in front of me and then to the side. There was only one.

Chapter 10: *SuKu - The Meeting*

She was wearing high-top boots, straw hat, and a cotton dress that fell just below the knees the day The Ted announced himself. The frock held snugly at The MaeAlice's hips and flapped against bare legs every time her arms swung the hoe. She had a rhythm, each motion deliberate and sure. Hoeing a row was familiar. It was how she saw her life; the rows were long, grass was plentiful. She kept the unearthed pieces of someone else's life in the pocket of the apron she wore. MaeAlice began tilling this plot of dirt right after her house was built. Alongside the men who helped prepare the land, she dug up tree stumps and roots buried deep as her misery.

She didn't see The Ted arrive. In her rhythm, She didn't hear him walk up behind her either. He tapped her shoulder. MaeAlice's rhythm was gone.

"Remember me?" he asked.

She stared at him, and went back to chopping. "I was here last night. With the guy you almost chopped in half with that ax of yours. Remember?"

A few more whacks at the ground and she responded, "Yeah, I remember," as if she thought it a stupid question.

The Ted assumed the words she didn't speak out loud: 'if you hadn't gotten him out of my house, you'd be planning a funeral.'

"I just came to apologize," he said. "I don't really know him. I'm visiting from Baltimore and hooked up with him through my friend, the other guy with us. Not knowing him don't change the fact that he showed his ass. That made me look bad so I want to say I'm sorry, and see if there's something I can do to make up for his insult."

The MaeAlice chopped through his monologue. Ted walked a slow pace behind between rows of beans she'd already chopped. At the end of that row, she turned to see The Ted holding his wallet and stared at it for a moment. MaeAlice dug the hoe into the soft, black earth and let it rest from her grip. She folded her knuckles on her hips and looked at him. Ted took money from his wallet. MaeAlice removed the straw hat with one hand and raised the tail of her dress with the other. She wiped her face, caring nothing that he was there.

The Ted looked uncomfortable in his city clothes at the end of a row of butter beans with a crisp bill in his hand.

21

He had stepped high and carefully to keep the dirt off his patent leather shoes, the same color of the earth, only shinier.

"Don't want nor need yo' money," The MaeAlice said, as she gripped the hoe from its resting place, and began the next two rows. Ted stepped across the beans to follow while keeping the dirt from sticking to his shoes.

"I'm sorry. I didn't mean to offend you," he said. "I just thought you being alone and raising all these children, you could use the money. Why don't you take it and buy them something. School starts in a couple of months, right? They'll need pencils and paper."

"Look, mister," she said, striking the hoe against the ground. "I don't know you, and you know nothing about what my chullen need. Now if you don't mind, I'm busy."

Ted stood still, holding a fifty-dollar bill. Finally, he folded the new money and pushed it inside his front pocket. "I guess I owe you another apology," he offered. "It's just that I think you're an amazing woman." He stopped for a moment, apparently to collect his thoughts.

"Truth is, I didn't come to apologize for that asshole. I was impressed with how you handled yourself and wanted an excuse to say so." Ted waited for her reaction. Getting none, he continued. "Fact is, there's something about you... I've never met a woman like you.... and probably never will again."

MaeAlice straightened her back and lifted her head to look into this man's face. She took him in: his jet-black hair slicked to his head like sealskin, a wave here and there rippled around his crown. He'd given the clump of hair at his forehead a slight lift.

Her eyes went to his white shirt, opened three buttons from the neck to reveal a fine shadow of chest hair shading his light brown skin. He looked like something fried perfectly. MaeAlice's Black-Indian skin was dark beside him. His sharkskin pants shone in the sun like his patent leather shoes. *Lonely Teardrops*, by Jackie Wilson, played on the radio perched on the pump house.

The MaeAlice asked him, "What do you want from me?" She must have recognized this man was at least twelve years younger, if not twelve years and a day. Whatever he said, she wasn't buying it.

"Did the cops send you?" she yelled. "Are you some kind of spook sent to spy on me? You want to lock me away for good? For what? Feeding my family?" That Mae-Alice had paid a small fine for bootlegging too many times fueled her suspicion.

"I'm no cop. I just want to get to know you. You are a woman who can use a man around. Let me do what I can."

"You want to help me?"

Ted nodded. He had taken the starched handkerchief from his back pocket and dabbed his face. It was two o'clock in the afternoon and the summer sun was very much on duty.

"Fine. Finish those last three rows of beans you standing in." She handed him the hoe.

The Ted tried speaking "But... but..." was all he could get out.

"If you want to help, then help. I say what help is." MaeAlice walked to house and was gone.

She came back with a tray of food and a small pitcher of lemonade. She carried the tray to the front yard and set it on a table. The flaps on the table's umbrella looked like giant tongues in desperate need of water. "Come here gal, keep the flies away." One sagging flap dragged Grace's head as she ducked underneath.

23

MaeAlice went back the garden. Ted's starched white shirt hung limp from the branch of a nearby tree. Sweat had stained the front and back of his tee shirt. The hand-kerchief he used to dab his face now wrapped his head to protect his hair from the dust he chopped up. The hoe knew it had no business in his hands and did little to coop-erate. He'd whack continuously before succeeding in sepa-rating the top of a weed from the bottom. The root stayed firmly in the ground.

The MaeAlice called to him without using his name. He'd said it, but she could not find it in her memory. "Put that down. And come get something to eat," she yelled.

The Ted looked at the end of the row just a few feet away. "I'm almost done," he called back. I'll be up in a minute," and went back to whacking the ground.

Grace sneaked a sip of his lemonade and watched him chop at the last few feet left to do. Luckily, the beans were densely planted. Ted anchored the hoe into the ground as he'd seen MaeAlice do. He took his shirt from the branch and followed her to the front yard. He bent and brushed dirt from his shoes as he walked. More than the beans and weeds, his shoes were the victims of his effort to be useful.

MaeAlice had fried pork chops, made rice and gravy, stewed squash and opened a can of store-bought biscuits. Ted didn't touch anything for a while. He excused himself to wash his hands at the pump near the back door. When he returned, he finally picked up the lemonade and drank. He put down the glass, and fumbled with his words.

"What's the matter, ya think I'd poison you," MaeAlice asked boldly.

"Uh, oh, no.... it's not that." Ted said.

"Then what?"

24

"Miss Mae, you went to a lot of trouble. I don't know how to say this. I mean, it really looks good and all... but...." Ted stopped in mid-sentence again.

"But what?"

"I don't eat pork."

MaeAlice snatched the plate from the table. "So, you're one of them. I've heard that nonsense y'all believe about pork. Demons cast into pigs. The Bible saying swine is unclean. That, I never understood. Of all the things in the Bible people want to follow. The same book said don't kill or lie. It said to honor your marriage. But every weekend, plenty who wouldn't put bacon to their mouths used those same lips on somebody else's husband, or whisper lies to somebody else's wife. Plenty of them take home vegetables from Mr. Jim's farm hidden in their coats or bring to me to pay their debt. Pigs feed my family and bring in money when I sell 'em. I have nothing whatsoever against pork." She stomped to the back door; it slammed behind her.

The Ted had put on his shirt and was about to leave when she returned with another plate. "Here's some leftover chicken from last night. You do eat chicken, don't-cha? Frankly, I'd take my chances with the pig. Chickens been known to eat shit. Pigs eat what I give em."

Ted apologized again. "I seem to have put you to some trouble. I didn't mean to do that. I wanted to meet you and hoped you'd let me come again. But obviously, I'm pushing my luck. I'll just go." And he did, leaving MaeAlice holding the plate of leftover chicken. It didn't occur to her at the time that she'd fried it in grease from the pig.

A week went by. The Ted returned with his friend. The fool almost hit in the head was not with them. Tonight, his golden fried skin looked like a sweet potato fresh from the oven. MaeAlice let him stay, gave him a drink on the house, and went on to the next customer. Late into the night, Ted made his way into the living room where she was making change for a fifty-cent drink.

"I don't allow people in here," she announced. "This is my house and it's not open to every Tom, Dick and Harry."

"I told you, my name is Ted. When I see Tom, Dick and Harry, I'll pass on the house rule," he said. "Why you so hard on me?"

"Look boy..."

"Boy?? What boy would you be talking to? There's only you and me that I can see."

"You young enough to be my child. What on earth do you want with me? Did the cops send you? You working for the man? Why else would you be playing games?"

The Ted walked up close and held her arms near the shoulders. He stared into her eyes for several minutes before he asked, "Does this answer your question?" He leaned forward and waited for her reaction. The MaeAlice did nothing. Without further notice, he kissed her. She heard that song again by Jackie Wilson, the one where his heart was crying...crying.

Chapter 11: *SuKu - Different*

The Ted's womanizing began the month after he put his suitcase underneath MaeAlice's bed. Her son was the first to hear. People came to him because at eighteen, he became the man of his mother's house. Daniel confronted Ted in the front yard where he lounged on the wooden swing. He did a lot of lounging, not much else. The Ted's feet stretched across the length of the swing and crossed at the ankles. Wrapped in a nylon scarf to protect the waves in his hair, his head rested on the flat arm of the swing. One arm tucked underneath for cushion, the other lay across his chest. His eyes were half shut from the view of the cemetery across the road where The Shelia Paxon, and a host of others lay dead. He stared at cheap tombstones of various shapes angled out of the grown like concrete weeds.

The Daniel confronted him. "The word is out on you."

"And what word is that?" The Ted continued his motion in the swing. The metal chain creaked as it moved back and forth. Daniel would have to fix that later; this business with Ted, he had to fix now.

When Daniel finished his telling, Ted opened his eyes fully and stared at him. His voice was calm and smooth. "You best mind your business, little country boy." He dropped one leg as if about to get up, but, instead, pushed against the ground to keep the swing in motion.

Daniel put his foot on the swing. The swaying stopped. The creaking held its breath. "My mother is my business," he said. "And if you hurt her with this bullshit people telling me, you'll know just how much my business it is." He lifted his foot from the swing and stepped away.

Ted did not respond. Instead, he leaned sideways, reached in his pants pocket, and withdrew a knife. He pulled back the metal, exposing a three-inch blade, and cleaned his fingernails.

The Daniel reached in the tree where he stood and broke a limb with one snap. He looked his enemy in the face—both understanding the other, neither backing down. Daniel threw the limb aside and walked away. Ted dropped one leg to the ground and pushed the swing off again. Screech... screeeech... scrrreeech...

It wasn't long before gossip landed on MaeAlice's ears again. She did what a woman who wants to hold onto the wrong man does. She ignored the truth. Accused every woman who brought news of being jealous, every man of wanting his place. The MaeAlice turned a deaf ear after severely cursing out whoever brought news about Ted, and then doubled her efforts to please him.

After a while, news of his behavior stopped coming. So did many of her customers. Friday and Saturday nights were different. Ted set the rules now and MaeAlice's regulars didn't like the rules he set. Business slowed. Jars of liquor went unopened. Lies men would fabricate about their sexual escapades went untold. MaeAlice accepted the changes and settled into the new conditions. Months had put the stories behind her. She had all but forgotten them entirely when one Saturday, around one in the morning, news came again. It was news she could not escape, from a messenger she could not ignore.

Chapter 12: *SuKu - Fear*

Her instincts had warned her. The MaeAlice had paced the house, looking for things she couldn't find and cursing because they weren't there. She didn't say much that day. She picked beans even though she'd done that chore the day before. Frost had come and the crops were almost done.

"Grandma, what's wrong," Grace asked, helping her turn over empty stalks. She, too, sensed dread but did not know its source. She saw the thing she could not name in her grandmother's face.

"Nothing, baby, nothing," was the reply as MaeAlice pushed the beanstalks aside, searching for what she might have missed, looking for what she could not find. Giving up, and not being able to shake the feeling that gripped her, she filled a bucket and washed every window.

The shadow of dread followed MaeAlice all day and into the night. Now, she couldn't sleep. As much as she tried to deny its presence, she had been like this before. It was followed by Death, come to fetch a passenger. It never left empty-handed.

The doorbell rang rapidly, followed by a series of frantic knocks. The MaeAlice pulled a curtain back from the window by her bed. "Slang?" she said to herself.

Slang was The Daniel's best friend. His name was Thomas Chester, but Slang is what everyone called him. He rarely spoke a sentence that was proper English. Almost everything he said was a rhyming cliché. He often made up words and dangled them in a sentence. People pretended to know what he meant, often nodded as contribution to his butchered conversation.

The oil lamp The MaeAlice always left burning when Ted or Daniel was out glowed softly. The ringing of the bell and the frantic knocks on the front door pane interrupted its glow. It was 1:28AM. MaeAlice did not move immediately, fear gripped her and held her still. She was uneasy all evening and had sent the last customer home just after midnight. She'd mopped the kitchen floor and laid down to rest. Now this panic at her door, fear rattling her window. The second series of knocks moved her.

Grabbing her housecoat, she stuck her feet in bedroom shoes made by walking on the heel of a pair of sneakers too small. She dragged them hurriedly down the hallway to the living room. Another series of agitated knocks echoed through the house. MaeAlice yelled, "Who is it!" even though she knew. Habit, perhaps. In reality, it was fear that made her ask.

"It's me, Miss Mae. Please open the door," the voice shouted back. "Mama Mae, please open the door!"

MaeAlice yelled through the wood that separated their conversation. "Is the police after you, boy?" She didn't bother to pull back the curtain covering the glass that had withstood his knocking.

Slang was known for breaking-in to stores late at night. He'd brought a pillowcase full of chicken, pork chops, steaks, and other meats from Buie's Grocery Store just a few nights ago. He didn't work anywhere so he paid his beer tab in trade. The St.John freezer was always stocked from the short line of credit MaeAlice extended him.

The Slang was a year younger than Daniel. He had finished his junior year of high school in May. Summer came and went. Unlike the rest of his classmates, he didn't go back when school started in September.

Slang lived down the road with his mother and two sisters. No father, like most of the children in the neighborhood. Both only sons, he'd been Daniel's best friend since they were ten years old. Slang had become a regular on Friday nights while he waited for Daniel to dress. This was October. In three months, she'd give him his first shot of moonshine. He'd be legal to drink hard liquor even though it was illegal for her to sell it. MaeAlice had warmed the stomachs of many young boys when they turned eighteen, free of charge. It would not be Slang's first drink of liquor; she knew that. But it would be the first he got from her. Besides, it was tradition. A boy wasn't a man until he had his inaugural drink from The MaeAlice's expert hand.

"Mama Mae! Oh lord, Miss Mae..." The voice was crying now. She fumbled at the locks, twisting them quickly. Slang rushed in past her and began pacing the vinyl-covered floor. He reached out to touch her, hold her, but she didn't like displays of affection. The oil lamp was low but she could see his shoulders were up to his ears like it was thirty degrees outside. His hands shook at the end of stiff arms. His eyes were wide. His lips trembled to speak but no words came out. Just sounds.

MaeAlice looked past him to see if someone was there. She didn't need the police on her doorstep tonight. She stuck her head outside and looked again. Slang had left the car lights on and the engine running. He'd parked inches from the steps leading to the porch. He'd almost hit the house. She pulled her head in and closed the door.

"Boy, what's wrong?" she asked, herself now agitated by his movements and the low moans in his throat. "Just stop!" she yelled at him. "Stop and tell me!"

MaeAlice spoke in commands; it always sounded as if you'd done something wrong. Were it not for Slang's behavior and the news he brought, nothing would be different. Except her fear. The news he brought tonight would feed upon her heart and change her forever.

Grace had followed her grandmother to the living room but stayed in the doorway off the hall. Only half her body was visible as she watched the two in this strange exchange. In the clearest sentence she had ever heard him speak, Slang said "Get dressed Miss Mae. We gotta go."

"Go where? Boy, what's wrong with you? You better tell me, and tell me now," she barked at him. He had scared her. Her voice said so.

"We gotta go to the hospital, Miss Mae. Daniel's been shot. Please Miss Mae. Get dressed so I can take ya. The car is running. We gotta hurry." These words came out of Slang's mouth, clean and precise. This was a mouth accustomed to saying things like 'Leave the jive in the hive', or, 'there's a woman out there just holding her britches, waiting for me... cause Slang is poppa-licious.'

The agitation MaeAlice had all day doubled. She rounded the corner to the hallway without touching the walls. Slang had told her to get dressed, but she didn't change. She put on a flannel shirt and pair of britches over what she was wearing and traded a pair of old sneakers for a pair of old shoes.

The front door slammed and the car backed out quickly from the driveway. Grace turned out the flicker from the oil lamp her grandmother had left burning. The blackened haze from the burning wick rested on the ceiling and lingered.

Chapter 13: *The Change*

It was 4:13AM when Grandmother returned. I must have dozed off because I awoke from hearing the front door open and the feet of several people drag across the floor. I crawled from the bed I shared with my sister, Lyn. Dillon had fought the covers in the other twin bed and won. The bedspread lay on the floor in a heap. I threw it across the little legs that sprawled like pick-up sticks.

In the living room, Slang and Aunt Olivia had placed Grandmother on the sofa and lifted her feet from the floor. The living room furniture was covered with plastic to protect the fabric from children and drunks. The plastic never mattered since neither was allowed in Grandmother's living room. Aunt Olivia had spread one of Grandmother's homemade quilts on the sofa to keep the plastic from clinging to her mother.

I heard Olivia say, "The tranquilizer will keep her out the rest of the night." She thanked Slang and closed the front door behind him. Aunt Liv pulled back the curtain and watched him drive away. She turned to see me standing in the hall.

Olivia sat in the armchair in the corner by the lamp. It was the only thing not covered in plastic. She hated the way the plastic sucked the skin like a leech and wouldn't let go. Once nestled in the chair, she took off her shoes. She liked high heels—the higher the better. Tonight, she'd worn her favorite pair and a tight dress split up the side. Most girls wore long, poodle skirts, but not Aunt Liv. A silver buckled belt showed off her small, contoured body. She wasn't as shapely as Grandmother but could hold a man's eye just the same. She pulled the dress up to her thigh so she could sit comfortably. The front of it was covered with a dark, dry substance. Her shoes lay on the floor stained in the same dark film. "Come her, baby," Aunt Olivia said tenderly. She reached out one arm and I walked towards her.

At twenty-three, Aunt Liv already had a child and had gotten married. In that order. She left her husband for beating her. That wasn't entirely true. She often pushed Uncle Charles into a fight and gave as well as she took. She had a scar across the front of her right shoulder blade from one of their fights. Uncle Charles wore a similar one from his left ear down to his neck. It was a mystery that such a little thing as Olivia, who weighed a hundred and ten pounds after eating, would go toe-to-toe with a man who cut down trees with a chainsaw for a living. What Uncle

Charles called protective, she called controlling. Aunt Olivia thought she was too young for an apron and a mop-- mother or not.

Seeing the dry blood, I thought my aunt had gotten into another fight with Uncle Charles for going out. Olivia liked nightclubs. Gyrating bodies finding their way to each other under the spell of colors bouncing off cut glass balls spoke to her. She said she liked the way the bass bounced off her ribcage and made it hard to breathe. Olivia loved the noise and laughter, the way everyone gave up the oppression they endured all week, at work and at home.

Aunt Liv had her mother's eyes. They were large and beautiful, deep and mysterious. As I climbed into her lap and looked into her face, I could see her aging that very moment. The powder that had stopped being make-up hours ago lay on her face like dust. Tears had washed a path down to her chin where it curved underneath and became lost in the shadow. Her faded lipstick reminded me of the chewy wax lips we bought for two cents each at Buie's Grocery Store. Just a faint hue of raspberry color remained.

"What's the matter Aunt Liv? Is Gran'ma okay?"

Olivia rested my head underneath her chin. "Shhhh," she whispered, gently fixing my nightgown around my body. Satisfied that I was protected, Olivia reached for the lamp, replaced its comfortless hue with the somber cover of darkness, and wept in silence.

Chapter 14: *SuKu - Sorrow*

The MaeAlice's sorrow was an endearing thing; a puppy found in snow. The tranquilizer did not still her sorrow. Low moans crept from her throat; her closed eyes still cried; trembling whimpers spilled from her throughout the night. Olivia and Grace kept watch over her restless body but we watched her soul; if not, she would have drowned in grief.

The preliminary report read: 'Died within minutes from a small caliber bullet to the back. It pierced the heart, hit a bone, ricocheted internally, and lodged in the liver.'

Around mid-morning, the police came to question MaeAlice about her son. Grace was feeding the chickens when the two cars arrived. Dillon helped; he liked throwing although his little arms didn't fling very far. Chickens ran to him pecking at his hand. Like he'd done before, he hid behind big sister. When the patrol car pulled into the driveway, Grace dropped the sack of corn and lifted Dillon off the ground. She sat him on the stump out of reach of the chickens. "Stay here," she instructed and ran inside. She knew what the men in these cars had done to MaeAlice on other visits they made. They came in the daytime; they came late at night; they came before sunrise in cars just like these. Sometimes they came just to issue a warning. On several of those visits they ransacked the house and took MaeAlice to jail.

Grace knelt down by the makeshift bed and told her they were coming. MaeAlice was coherent but still dazed. On one of few occasions, MaeAlice whispered in a voice that came from a distant place, "It's ok."

When the doorbell rang, The Grace answered it. One
of the policemen asked, "Is MaeAlice home?" He didn't
say Miss MaeAlice or Mrs. St. John, just MaeAlice.

"She's not feeling well," Grace answered.

The same one spoke again. "We need to talk with her."

By now MaeAlice has gotten up from the couch and
faced a man she had not seen before. She watched the two,
taking in the new face through the locked screen door. As
best she could, she put the new face in memory; sure she'd
see it again.

They never asked to come in; she never invited them.
She knew them. Despite the nature of their visit, she did
not trust them. The third officer walked to the back of the
house. MaeAlice knew him best. He had taken her to jail
on several occasions for selling liquor without a license.
He'd handcuffed her and dragged her by the crook of her
arm to his patrol car. The back of her heels dug furrows
from the back door steps to the front of the house. She
kicked dirt and spat at him, falling at least twice along the
way.

One of these at the front door she also knew by name.
He had gone through her cupboard and dropped jars of
canned fruit to the floor. Three jars of peaches and one of
watermelon marmalade lay open on the floor. Juice the
children missed when cleaning up had dried in a corner by
the time MaeAlice returned. So, not even now, under this
circumstance, could she invite them into her home.

"It appears…" He hesitated and looked at his pad for
a name …"Daniel was killed in an argument with an unknown assailant," one said.

"Did your son have an altercation with anyone?" the
other asked.

"Grace, come get your brother," Olivia called. She was putting the finishing pat on a pan of biscuits for breakfast. Lyn helped her dab butter on top. The Olivia had seen them coming; she expected them. Through the kitchen window, she watched the third officer lift wood from the pile with his foot. He watched as Dillon tossed grains of corn one at a time. The officer stared at him. He lifted the bag of corn Grace had dropped and dumped half of it to the ground. He rummaged through the rest then patted Dillon's head.

Olivia swung open the kitchen door and stomped out in bare feet. The door banged loudly against the joist before resting in place. The officer turned to see her within inches of his back.

"Unless you're looking for my brother's killer in that sack, you'd better have a search warrant in your pocket to do anything else." Olivia stood flat with flour on her face and a knife pointing from a clenched fist on her hip. She had put on one of MaeAlice 's daisy print housecoats. The thin wrap swallowed her and swelled from the early breeze. She looked as fierce as she sounded. Her frazzled short hair spiked on top of her head like hundreds of spiders arched for battle; her eyes bloodshot from crying and lack of sleep. Spit flew from her mouth and nearly landed on his crisp brown sleeve.

The sun shone on the officer's name badge and made her squint but she didn't look away. Olivia didn't ask his name and he didn't offer. The look on her face conveyed she didn't care. The officer rested his hands on his gun belt, lifted the load, and walked away. A dozen pullets and four roosters squawked and flapped over each other to collect the grains of corn he'd dumped in a heap.

The officer met up with the other two as they left the porch. Neither had asked The Olivia any questions. She wouldn't have told them what she knew if they had. What would they do? They didn't care about MaeAlice's grief or her murdered son.

The third officer arrived in time to hear his partner say, "Sorry for your loss," without adding the customary "ma'am," to show respect.

MaeAlice watched their car doors close and the black vehicles with no hubcaps roll backward from her driveway. Although this visit was different, it had a strange familiarity. They did not take her away physically, but they left with something of her all the same.

The Olivia took Dillon from the stump, "go help feed the pigs," she said, lightly spanking his bottom. She watched him run, his curly hair catching the sun. Seeing the officer standing over him made her skin itch. She rubbed her arm with deliberate motion, up and down. She returned to the kitchen and finished breakfast. Lyn helped her to bring bacon, eggs, and grits to MaeAlice with a cup of thick coffee and biscuits fresh from the oven.

MaeAlice sat in the corner of the sofa using the chair's arm to prop her. She looked at the food on the serving tray and closed her eyes. When Olivia looked in after feeding the children, the food sat on the tray as she'd left it. "Why didn't you eat?" she scolded. "I heard you in here asking God for strength. Well, here it is. Eat." Olivia reminded her mother that things needed to be done. Arrangements had to be made.

Chapter 15: *SuKu - The Nightmare*

"Lord, Olivia! It's your brother! He's been shot" Those three sentences looped in her head. The Slang knew who did it. He told the story to Olivia that night at the hospital after he'd delivered MaeAlice there. Olivia had bits and pieces; Slang filled in the gap. She had been at Jesse's Place that night, the nightclub where Daniel was shot. Like everyone else, she heard the gunfire and ran towards the door.

The words hit and froze her still. She heard them far, far away; the girl's mouth stretched across her face and her eyes glazed with tears. Finally, the words reached her; they boomed on Olivia's heart and resonated until she felt them, tight in her chest.

There was a crowd around Daniel when she reached the spot where he had fallen. He lay in a heap like a broken toy. One arm reached out into the darkness. She could see the puddle of blood. The earth beneath sipped his life, tasted his youthful vigor, soaked-in his story. The Olivia held both hands across her mouth. She dropped to her knees, lifted Daniel's face from the dirt and held his head in her lap. She rocked his body amid screams that tore from her throat. The police and ambulance had been called. Sirens shrilled in the distance. The night air mingled their sounds with her screams, blending each with the other until they were one.

The Slang came running back from a path in the woods behind the club. His body shook like a man whose whole life disturbed him. His voice trembled but he spoke clearly. "I'll go get Miss Mae and meet you at the hospital. I can't be here when the police come; I got a gun." He waited for some sign that she heard him. "Don't worry Liv, I'll get that son-of-a bitch." With that, he sped towards a mother awaiting a visit with death.

~ o ~

Slang and Olivia sat in his car outside the hospital. She listened as he retold the events that had brought them here. He and Daniel were trolling for girls. Daniel had turned nineteen in August. Girls loved his thick curly hair and mystic brown eyes. Older women did, too. Slang got action because he was Daniel's friend. A car drove up that they recognized. So was the woman who sat in the passenger's seat.

"It was one of them ushers from church," Slang said. "I can't think of her name. She was at Miss Mae's house yesterday. She claims to be Miss Mae's friend…" Slang paused, clenching his teeth on the words.

"Daniel saw her in the car and started cussing. I tried to hold him back, and did for a while, till the two of 'em started laughing. Daniel thought they was laughing at him." Slang stopped speaking for a moment. "If she hadn't laughed…" He stopped again, holding his breath as he collected the rest of the night from somewhere in his head. "Why he wanna bring his bitch to that place?" He wasn't speaking to Olivia; he was asking the question to fate.

"Who!" Olivia asked. It was a two-part question. She wanted the name of the man who dared to do what he did, and the woman in the middle of it. She thought Slang was talking about a man dating one of Daniel's girlfriends, except she didn't know of any usher he dated, nor what woman was at her mother's house the day before.

40

Slang started talking again. "Liv, I swear, I didn't know this was gonna go down." Another silent pause held back his journey to truth.

"Goddammit," she said, "what the fuck are you telling me? Whatever it is, you better tell it quick!"

Slang didn't seem to hear her. If he did, he wasn't compelled by her frustration. He thought how much she sounded like MaeAlice. Olivia heard him breathe—a long draw of the crisp night air. It sneaked in through cracks he made in the car's back windows, touching them both. He sucked in as if inhaling a cigarette.

"He's dead, ya know," Slang confessed. "I'm seventeen. Might not see eighteen after tonight. He was my best friend. I gotta take care of this. I gotta set things right."

"You're right, you won't see eighteen cause I'll kill yo' ass right here, right now if you don't tell me what the hell you talking about!"

The threat snapped Slang back to the fact that she was in the car and he was telling her what happened. "I'm sorry, Liv. It's just… that… I can't wrap my head 'round this thang. I don't want to believe it's true. But we're both sitting here in front of a hospital where your brother lay dead, and yo mama is being shot full of dope to help her through it."

"Liv, I tried to stop it. You gotta believe me. That's why I wasn't there when you found him. I ran that son-of-a-bitch into the woods. I tried my best to kill him but he got away."

Slang picked up the pace. "Me and Daniel tried to pay 'em no mind. But Daniel thought he heard that woman call yo mama's name. That's when we heard the laughing. Daniel went to the car. He started cussing the woman and told her not to ever set foot at his house again. He said, 'I'll

41

kick your ass back to that roach-infested rat trap you call home.' The man told him to shut the fuck up. They yelled back and forth. Daniel told him not to set foot at your mama's house again either or he'd kill him. He said, 'you'll find yo' shit at this bitch's house.'"

The Olivia's heart raced; her voice found another pitch. Are you telling me... are you telling me..." she didn't finish the sentence. Slang's nod said she didn't have to.

"He said in this calm voice, 'If anybody's leaving, it'll be you, you little bastard.' He leaned back in his car seat and sucked on this big ass cigar. Then he said, in this arrogant tone... Slang stopped and squirmed. "Excuse me for saying this Olivia but it's what he said." He paused again and let go the words. "He said, 'Your stupid ass mama wants what I got so bad she signed over her house to me. I own it. So tomorrow, you get the fuck out. That's my house and your mama might go with you if you ain't careful. You'll be on your knees in front of me doing what she did last night if you wanna keep a roof over her head.' We both knew he was fucking with Daniel, but to say that... "

Slang stopped again. The words were foul in his mouth. He frowned after saying them. Unconsciously, he rolled down his window and spat. He wiped his mouth on his sleeve and went on.

"Daniel reached down and grabbed up a Coke bottle. He broke the window where the woman was. Eva Lee.... that's her name. Eva Lee.... Anyway, glass flew everywhere. Daniel snatched the woman out of the car across the broken glass, punched her with his fist and slung her to the ground. I'd never seen him hit a woman before. He punched her like she was a man. He knocked her clear off the ground. One of her shoes flew to one side and she landed on some rocks on the other. She was all scraped up, cussing, and crying. He musta broke her nose cause blood was pouring between her fingers when she rolled over. Then he reached in the car to drag out that bastard, but Ted had opened his car door and fell on the ground. Daniel ran to the other side of the car in time to grab him. He started beating the shit outta him. Daniel knocked him to the ground, kicked him in the back and stomped him." The Slang stopped again. Remembering.

"I never seen nobody that angry. His eyes looked like hot charcoals. "I wudda helped him stomp that son-of-a-bitch but he didn't need no help. Whatever burned in him needed to get free. After a while, I went over to pull Daniel off him. I grabbed him around the chest in a bear hug but he pushed my arms apart like I was a two-year-old child. I fell. By the time I got up, Daniel had found a piece of two-by-four from where they were fixing up the club. He started beating that car till the board broke. Liv, I swear, there was these sounds coming from him like I never heard befo'. Animal sounds -- grunt'n... mean noise. He went crazy. Something had hold of him, Liv. If vengeance has a face, it had to look like Daniel did right then.

The next thing I know, I hear the shot. Daniel starts to fall. He dropped the board in his hand. Ted was up and running. I picked up a piece of the board and threw at him, but missed. It was dark and he disappeared into the bushes. I ran to my car and got my gun. I chased him through the woods. I fired a few shots but he was hiding in the bushes or had got away. He didn't fire on me I guess 'cause Daniel had messed him up pretty good. He might've passed out but it's so thick back there I couldn't find him. That's when I ran back and found you holding Daniel." Slang took another long deep breath.

43

Neither Slang nor Olivia spoke again that night. They sat silently, feeling the bite of a black, October chill. Fearful that whatever sprang from Daniel that night, would find them, too.

Chapter 16: *Nola*

"Maybe if you'd kept your ass home, my brother might not be dead. He was only nineteen years old. You're the oldest in this family, Nola. And where were you?" Aunt Olivia hurled the question at my mother. "You had to run. Hm-mpf, you think you the only one here who needs to forget?" I wondered what that meant but couldn't ask because I wasn't supposed to be there.

Mama was home for the funeral. It felt strange to see her. Except for the fancy New York hairdo she called a French twist she looked the same. But her being here didn't feel same. Three years had passed. Dillon didn't know her. He was only four when she left. Lyn hid behind me to watch her. Despite these facts, our southern upbringing ensured her our respect. We called her mama, said yes-ma'am, and did what we were told.

As often as possible, I found something that needed doing elsewhere when she approached me. I fed the chickens, raked the yard, swept the porch. Often, I'd busy myself away from the house with a book after I'd finished the self-appointed chores. Busy work with "the arrangements" made it easier. Not knowing what that meant at first, I thought it must be bad because Mama and Aunt Olivia argued about it constantly. Grandmother cried every time they brought it up.

"You're still a street cat," Mama declared about her sister. "Don't matter what it is, you just go straight at it... don't even think about what's coming out of your mouth."

Olivia snapped back. "You're some big city shit now, what do you care about what happens here?" It was a question demanding an answer. "You left your own flesh and blood here. What arrangements did you make for them? Maybe you think you can take care of the dead better than you can the living." It was meant to cut and did. The corners of my lips curled slightly in satisfaction.

Mama's fury slammed pots onto the cast iron stove. She slung food onto plates and sat chairs down harder than necessary, then reminded Olivia, "I'm here now and I 'am' the oldest. I told them what Mama and I want, and that's what's gon' be. If you have a problem with that, tell it to whoever cares what you think."

The program would be done as Mama instructed. No matter the fight Olivia put up, according to our culture, that was that. Having had her say, Mama left the room. Quickly. She knew Olivia's next move might be towards her with whatever was in her hand. More than that, she needed to escape Aunt Liv's words. Mama sat on the bed and rocked, calming her anger, trying to push back whatever was coming for her. As she wiped her eyes with the towel across her shoulder, Dillon pulled her blouse. She had not seen him come in.

"Mommy," is all he said.

Chapter 17: *Paying Respect*

The funeral was scheduled for Friday at 1:00 PM. At the wake on Thursday, the St.John house spilled with people who came to pay respects. They bought food and prayers. The wreath of white chrysanthemums with olive-green foliage hung by the front door as dead as Daniel. The funeral home would use it again to announce the departure of some other dearly departed.

No one rang the doorbell; they simply pulled open the screen door and came inside. I watched them from the swing in the front yard. They laughed and joked past the long line of cars and made their way to the house. Tones changed to a mouth full of sorrow as they reached the door.

Inside, they'd say, "Lord, honey, I'm so sorry for your loss. This is a terrible thing, but God knows best."

They found their way to the kitchen to hand over a bowl to Mama or Olivia. Most brought macaroni and government cheese. Potato salad was a favorite, too. After that came pinto beans, and collard greens, both flavored with heaping chunks of fatback. If meat showed up it was chicken or meatloaf. Most everyone in Blessing struggled to make ends meet. We understood their selections. The dishes were inexpensive, easy to prepare and filling. They'd also safely keep for at least three days.

Many of the women who brought their offering in repurposed containers didn't even like Grandmother. But at a time like this, it was proper they pay respects. So, they came, bearing plastic bowls covered in plastic wrap with their name written on the container so they'd be sure to get it back.

Mama continued cooking. Grandmother didn't allow us to eat anything that wasn't prepared by a St.John. Just as Grandmother could make anything grow, Mama could cook. This was her physical gift. The recipes were in her head and her hands measured everything. She could create flavors from the most unlikely ingredients that made you close your eyes just to savor the moment.

So, the chain of plastic bowls was laid out for the visitors who served themselves on paper plates and ate with plastic forks. They wiped their mouths with paper napkins and drank from paper cups.

Chapter 18: *The Visit*

Olivia came looking for me in the grove of trees in the cemetery. The view must have bothered her. She put a hand on a tree to steady herself, then rounded the huge oak that spread its limbs across the community of the dead.

She sat beside me on the ground. "They were getting on my nerves, too."

I smiled. She took my hand, rubbed it between her own, and waited for me to talk. "Aunt Liv, I was thinking about when you taught me how to jump rope and play jacks. You even played house with me and we made mud pies over there."

"I remember," Olivia said. "We made beds out of sacks filled with straw, and used paint buckets for chairs. Uncle Charles built us a table. He was always bringing home scrap wood. We couldn't burn it all. MaeAlice tried. There was so much of it she built houses for her pigs."

We both laughed at the idea. Houses for pigs. Olivia patted my thigh. We filled the space with silence, remembering something that could easily have happened last week as it did two years ago. So much had changed and it wouldn't change back. The chain of events that brought us to this spot was permanent and we knew it.

"Aunt Liv, you remember that tea set you gave me? It wasn't even my birthday. I loved that tea set more than anything I ever got."

"Tell me what's on your mind, Grace."

She knew. Aunt Olivia was not a first-born, but certainly got some of what was gifted to the women who were. I started slowly, "Uncle Daniel came to the house that night."

"What night?"

"The night he died."

"What do you mean?"

"It was before Slang came to get Grandma. I was asleep and felt something tug my toes. I thought it was Dillon. But when I sat up, Uncle Daniel was at the foot of the bed. He looked at me but didn't say anything at first. I thought he was just checking on us, making sure we were asleep. I was going to lay back down but he called my name."

"He talked to you?" Olivia asked.

"Well, not exactly. I mean, he didn't talk talk. His mouth didn't move, but he said, 'tell Momma I'm all right; Tell her not to worry. Everything is as it should be.' I said ok. Then, he said 'go back to sleep now.' Uncle Daniel didn't smile a lot since Ted came, but he smiled.

"After a while, Slang came. I heard Grandma scream, kinda. Then she left with Slang. When she came back she was crying and you were with her. Now all these people are coming, talking about Daniel and Grandma. Since that night I've been afraid to tell her what he said. But if he said he's all right, how can he be dead?"

"Are you sure you saw Daniel that night, sweetie? Are you sure?"

"Yes, Aunt Liv. I'm sure."

Chapter 19: *SuKu – The Wake*

Dozens of people filled the wooden box that sat atop rows of cinder blocks. It was the first and largest of a dozen scattered down the dirt road that was Tate Street. Its white, wooden planks, with green shutters, would have stood out in the neighborhood on its own, but The MaeAlice had whitewashed the trees. Against the leaves, some turning orange, red, and gold, the house made a spectacular view. A few hours ago it looked more dressed for a party than a wake. For the moment, it sounded like a party, too. Laughter echoed from everywhere, inside the house and out.

The wake would start soon. A prayer for the living would be offered and songs sung to invite compassionate spirits. People would remember The Daniel and tears would fall in regret for a life gone too soon. Then food would be passed around so that all in attendance could eat the sins of the dead. The Estelle Samuda knew this. She watch the visitors fill their plates till there was no more room, and wondered if they knew. Wine was absolution; in this case it was tea. Everyone there, with a plate in hand, had, perhaps unknowingly, agreed to eat the sins and atone the wrongs The Daniel had committed during his lifetime. At the rate they were consuming, Daniel's passage would be easy.

The MaeAlice was dressed in black from head to toe. A veil trimmed in velvet covered her face. She sat in the side chair, the one where Olivia had held Grace the night that Daniel had died. Churchwomen, dressed in white, surrounded MaeAlice. Some sat in folding chairs on both sides of her, others stood behind. They placed hands on her shoulders, and whispered in her ear. Their comfort looked hostile, as if their goal was to press the bereaved deeper into sadness. The MaeAlice looked broken. Her body slumped. For many, this was the first time seeing her helpless and frail, pitiful and deplete. Grief covered her like a cloaked vampire drinking her rational mind.

Daniel was her only son. His parents gave him their names to honor their achievement, pronouncing him to the world as Daniel Malice St.John. When asked about her husband, all MaeAlice would say is, "He died too soon." Not many knew the circumstance of his death, but they all came to the same conclusion—MaeAlice loved him. And now Daniel would join his father, dead too soon.

The Daniel was handsome from any set of eyes. His bronze-skin featured the Indian heritage evident in his dark, curly hair. A two-year-old mustache rested like an ornament above his lips. His nineteen-year-old body had begun its transformation to manhood. His chest was solid and his arms strong. Lying in the casket, he looked artificial, like the white wreath on The MaeAlice's front door. His chest was too high. The suit looked too big. But all who passed by said he looked natural. "Thompson sure did a good job," they said.

The house had emptied, except for The Estelle Samuda who stayed to help clean up. Paper plates and plastic forks were found everywhere. Olivia found a paper cup tucked behind the cushion on the sofa. "Trifling bastards," she said out loud, and looked under every other cushion for the remnants of other trifling bastards. For the first time, she was glad for the plastic covers.

Estelle Samuda took MaeAlice to her room and helped her undress. Estelle was from Trinidad, had known Daniel St.John since they were barefoot children. His mother had given Estelle instructions to find him when she arrived in New York. He would help her get settled in her new land. When he left New York he sent for her to come.

"Life is simple here," he told her. "The people remind me of home. They grow their own food and help one another. You would like this place." She followed him to Blessing.

Estelle Samuda knew how MaeAlice must feel but would not allow herself to think on it too deeply. She'd witnessed this same emptiness in this same face when Daniel St.John had died. His death had brought them closer together. Only the two of them knew it was MaeAlice's jealousy over the other that Daniel St.John was dead. She had reason. The bond of Trinidad, an ache for their culture had changed how they saw one another. All the same, after Daniel's death, the two women formed a deeper friendship over time. They relied on each other.

After undressing her, Estelle Samuda hung MaeAlice's clothes and tucked her in bed. She gave her one of the light blue pills that would help her sleep, rubbed her forehead, and left.

The pill half-worked. Behind flickering eyelids, Mae-Alice replayed every significant moment of Daniel's life as she remembered it: his birth, his first word, when he learned to walk. She remembered every event through the day she first noticed his mustache.

She did not play the times he took her whiskey money or argued with her about Ted. MaeAlice could not show affection in her waking world, under sedation, she cried into her pillow and smiled every once in a while when a memory allowed her to forget, for a brief second, that her Daniel was dead.

Olivia sat alone in the living room after everyone had gone. The Nola was staying with friends. The body was back at the mortuary. She would sit with MaeAlice tonight, volunteering for the duty.

Olivia knew part of her mother's grief was intertwined with Ted's absence. Tonight, she would tell her mother the truth; she could not let this woman bury her son tomorrow with needful thoughts in her heart of the man responsible for his death.

Having taken off her shoes some time ago, Olivia walked through the house locking doors and turning out lights. In the kitchen, she found the hiding place and poured herself a drink of rum and Coke. She felt it radiate in her stomach and spread to her limbs. She sighed and took a smaller drink for fortitude, then headed to her mother's room.

Despite the pain she knew it would cause, The Olivia felt avenging with her news. She despised Ted as much as anyone and hated that MaeAlice put this man before her family and friends. "Lord, help me find the words to do this," she prayed. The sedative should have kicked in by now, she thought. That should make it easier for her to handle.

An oil lamp burned low on the dresser in the corner. The room had an electric lamp but MaeAlice preferred the oil—she found the flicker comforting. Olivia quietly lifted one of the wooden chairs the church sisters had used and placed it at the bed. MaeAlice's eyes were closed. Tears had dried a path across her cheeks. Olivia reached for the cloth on the bedpost, wet it with the water from the glass on the nightstand and dabbed her mother's face. She stroked the flesh until MaeAlice groaned. She whispered, just loud enough for her mother to hear. "Momma, I need to talk to you... Momma, can you hear me, wake up. We need to talk."

Since she was seventeen years old, The Olivia spoke to MaeAlice as an equal. She felt moving out of her mother's house gave her that privilege. Of her mother's children, she knew she was liked the least.

The MaeAlice rolled her head in Olivia's direction. The sedative was working but did not ease the gruff in her voice when she saw her daughter. "What do you want," she drooled. "Leave me be."

Olivia tried to ignore that even now, her mother's words were vinegar. "Momma, I have to talk to you."

"Get out, leave me be."

"No! You're going to hear what I have to say. You need to know this and you're going listen." Olivia snatched her hand from her mother's arm. "Did you sign over this house to Ted?"

"What business is that 'yorn?" The words came like cold molasses.

The compassion Olivia had summoned raced down her throat and sizzled when it hit the rum. She drew a deep breath, pressed her back against the wooden slats, and repeated the story Slang had told the night her brother died. She told The MaeAlice about the car and the usher in the front seat. She told how Daniel heard the man and the woman laughing. That The Ted planned to put MaeAlice out of her own house. She left out nothing, not even the part about making love to her made him want to puke. MaeAlice rolled her head in sedated denial. Olivia rushed to the finish line.

"Daniel got into a fight with that bitch Eva Lee and Ted. He listened to that son-of-a-bitch you brought into this house say how stupid you are, how you beg him to touch you. Ted was with another woman, using your money." Olivia told the whole story. When she was done, her voice had lost its edge but the words were razor sharp. "Daniel was defending you, Momma. And it's because of you that he's dead."

The MaeAlice growled in her throat. It was not a loud, wretched scream. Nothing close. The sound she made was deep, and guttural. It went through the house like a blind cat finding its way in the dark. The cold inside MaeAlice cracked, letting something loose from way deep. Whatever it was rode on the sound from her throat and turned into stabbing metal once it left her mouth. It did not falter even when it saw the damage it caused. Instead, stuck tightly into Olivia's chest. It had deeper to go.

Chapter 20: *SuKu – The Procession*

A long black limousine sat in the St.John driveway, waiting. Inside the house, family rushed around doing last minute things families in Blessing do for the only event that lets them sit in luxury, on baby smooth leather, and feel important.

The MaeAlice was ready. She looked mysterious in her midnight attire. The dress covered her like a fitted shroud, hugging her frame. Where the dress stopped midway her calves, sheer black hosiery took over. Her half-inch heels with the fake diamonds brought the appropriate attention to her legs. A pillbox hat draped with a sheer black veil covered all but her lips and chin. It's satin rim arched around her face and rested on her shoulders. The MaeAlice never looked more beautiful. Sorrow became her. Behind the veil, sad eyes held two terrible facts. She would bury her only son today. And the man she loved had killed him.

Olivia tied ribbon on plaits and ponytails. Nola clipped bowties on little boys who stretched their necks and squinted their eyes. Each set of children fidgeted, unsure why they were forced into their Sunday clothes on Friday. Each had taken a note to school three days before informing of death in the family. The notes were unnecessary. Everybody knew that, today, MaeAlice would lay her son to rest.

The funeral director arrived in the longest of three limousines. He backed the stretch within inches of the bumper of another that was in place a half-hour before. The director made his way through the maze of people in every cranny of the yard. He didn't knock; his presence was expected. Inside, The Mr. Thompson tipped his Derby to the crowd in the living room, and held it comfortably under his arm.

He stood silently to announce his presence. When the chatter subsided, he said. "I'd like to go over the procession, if I may." His words were clear. He presented his image as if it were a sacred façade handed down. Despite the theatrics, his voice and mannerisms were sincere.

Mr. Thompson, the third, gathered his breath and spoke his last sentence on the process. "The minister will direct the immediate family to the seats around the burial site. All others will stand." He paused to give those present another moment of reflection. Seeing all were in accord, he turned and walked slowly to the sad creature. He extended his arm and helped her to her feet. Letting go of his image for a moment, he whispered, "Miss Mae, I am so sorry." His voice was as pure as the earthly depth from which it came. A small spasm heaved her chest and escaped as a moan behind pursed lips. Her head drifted to his waiting shoulder.

A young girl made her way to this mother in pain. Her eyes were glassy with tears as she spoke. "Ms. St.John, my name is Denise York. I loved your son."

Chapter 21: *SuKu – The Funeral*

It was two-ten when the procession arrived at Dew Well Baptist Church. The sun was warm and the leaves vibrant with color. The drive took the motorcade through a grove of trees like sentry lining both sides of the road. Branches reached for each other across the highway like members in a high wire act. The glassy black limousines caught the sturdy trees' reflections and mirrored back their splendor. The wind tickled the gold and amber leaves causing them to titter. Crimson, gold, and brown, they fell, dancing on the wind like snowflakes. It was a beautiful day for going home.

The church bells tolled announcing the family's arrival. The Nola stood on the right of her mother as they ambled up the sidewalk. At least sixty people lined the walkway. Those behind them stretched their necks and leaned either way to get a clearer view. A hundred others sat inside, having arrived early to ensure a seat. The doors of the church were opened. The Minister had said this phrase countless times as he invited people to loose their sins at the Alter, and take up the cross of Jesus. Those on the end of each pew leaned to look out the opened door to see the bereaved. As the bells rang, the organist played. Many expected The Nola to sing but the program did not mention it. A slow chord of "Precious Lord" trailed through the open doors and filled the yard outside. The mournful sound of each note rested on the hearts of those who really listened. The minister rested one palm atop the pages of the passage he read.

"To everything there is a season and a time and place for everything under the sun. A time to plant and a time to pluck up that which is planted, A time to laugh and a time to cry. A time to live and a time to die..."

The pallbearers had reached the top of the six steps of Dew Well Baptist Church. Another set of six on the side door combined to represent the twelve disciples. The Mae-Alice looked up to see her only son carried by six of his friends into a church he rarely attended, to be eulogized by a man he barely knew. Daniel was dead, killed by the man she put in his way. She trembled at the thought. A moan like the one she wrestled before escaped her throat. The same October breeze that danced with the leaves along the drive, brushed past Nola and lifted MaeAlice's veil just enough to allow a lone, solemn tear to fall, uninterrupted.

Chapter 22: *SuKu – The Aftermath*

The festivities after the funeral lasted well into the night and began their descent late Saturday evening. For two days, aunts and uncles, cousins—first, second, third, and those too distant to claim—filled the little white house on Tate Street. Fish was fried in the black wash pot. Cheap beer was drunk from coolers inside and outside the house. Children played and fought. Mothers yelled and spanked. Stomachs cramped from laughter and heads got pushed aside playfully. Groups huddled in the yard soaking up the last autumn sun, closing the gap in time. Then it was over.

Things were different; the family was forever changed. The Olivia's presence in Blessing was one of those things. She was leaving with her uncle going north. She didn't bother to divorce Charles. He wouldn't have agreed anyway. She didn't tell her mother good-bye; the two had not spoken since the night of the wake. She had no regret and The MaeAlice would never take back. Their relationship would fade in the distance with every white line that passed Olivia's eyes along the way to thirty-one years of separation.

Olivia piled her things into the big blue Cadillac that Sunday afternoon. It wasn't much—three small suitcases, a box of knick-knacks and her three-year-old son. The Grace had gone to her favorite spot in the cemetery while Olivia packed her life. Daniel was not buried here; the family plot was several miles away. She knew these occupants only by the names on their tombstone. And now, they were the only ones in which she could confide. She went to them knowing Olivia would come looking. She spotted Shelia

Paxon's tombstone midway the granite forest. She laid her sweater on the ground and sat down. She pulled her knees up and tucked her dress underneath.

A company of black ants came by and sniffed. Scouts. She'd watched this ritual a hundred times. As expected, they crawled over the knitted acrylic and continued their search for food. A bug buzzed her head. She slapped it. Dazed, it flapped on the ground trying to recover. With a small twig, she pinned the nuisance by its wing. A member of the ant brigade came along. Grace laid the intruder along the ant's path. The scout stopped and turned in the trapped prey's direction. His antenna wiggled. The bug was soon covered with a pulsating black mound. He tried desperately but did not escape.

While Grace watched the bug succumb to its fate, Olivia called her name. She envisioned her aunt scanning the cemetery in her search to say good-bye.

"Grace......Grace, baby........ Graaace........."

The Olivia waited. There was no jumping out from around the big oak tree like when they played hide-and-seek. Silence followed. Grace watched the ants carry the bug away in pieces. Something whole now in pieces, carried away. Minutes passed. Then it was Olivia's name being carried by the wind in the voice of Uncle Book. "Come on gal... long road ahead."

Seconds passed. Grace heard the crinkle of leaves under Olivia's feet beginning thirty-one years of distance. She pulled her knees closer, locked her arms around them, and wept.

Chapter 23: *Reunion*

I kept my gaze on Ted at the foot of Grandmother's bed. Her hand had stopped shaking inside my palm. Droplets of water glistened in the corner of her eyes. Her body wanted to cry but she denied it. I didn't know if it was pure will or there wasn't enough strength in her body to force the droplets down. "It's been a while," I said to him.

"Yes, you're all grown up," Ted answered. "Just look at you; the afro is a nice touch."

I'd been told many times that I looked like the actress Pam Grier. It was more than the hair; we had many features I common. Even so, I ignored his compliment. Neither did I ask the obvious question; he'd tell me why he was here. Or something. They always did. I'd learned not to waste energy on the dead. They had their own agenda.

"She's not giving up, is she?" he said, looking at Grandmother. "Don't blame her. That's one of the things I liked about Mae, she's a fighter. Has a mean streak the size of the Atlantic, but a survivor. Always made her own way; didn't matter what anyone thought or said. You'd do well to walk in your own shoes, too, Grace. Your grandmother certainly did. Learn from her."

Wasn't he here to tell his version of what happened? If not, why? And how could Grandmother see him? Dementia, I assumed. It opened all kinds of doors for her. People long ago dead returned to sit with her. Some she knew and remembered. Others she didn't. Some laughed with her; some held conversations. Ted's visits made her cry.

"What do you suggest I model? Her mean streak, perhaps?"

Ted smiled Ted's smile. I noticed he had not changed in the thirty-odd years since I saw him last. Did death stop time or was he showing me what I would remember? Looking at him now, with adult eyes, I could see why Grandmother wanted him.

But I had questions that had nothing to do with him, or her, that none of the others I'd encountered would answer. They'd conduct their business and leave me with curiosity. Rarely did they tell me anything I wanted to hear. Like, 'what's it like being dead? What do you do all day? What's the point of life?' They never talked about that. So, why was he here?

I waited. As usual, this visit was not for me; the visitors talked; I listened.

"Lots of questions, still," he said. "I have come to understand many things, Grace. But, unlike the Voices you hear, I have no wisdom to impart, only a view from my reality."

"You know about Them?" I didn't know who they were; they never said. But they *knew* things.

"Yes, I know about the Sisters, Grace," Ted answered. "They protect you. Often from yourself. By the way, the name you gave them is close enough."

That comment triggered a memory, as if Ted had willed it. I had named them long ago, and had almost forgotten. When I first heard the voices they were like thoughts in my head, only I knew they were not from me.

I was having a bad day at work the first time they appeared. My boss knew I was a single mom and needed the job. Went out of his way to break my spirit, to turn me into a copy of the other women who gave up and gave in. Most of my employees were white men. Some respected me. Most didn't. It was the seventies and black women in in-

61

dustry, except as assembly workers, were oddities. My manager all but called me incompetent even when I followed his instructions. But someone had to be blamed for his ignorance. When the department manager pissed on him, he pissed on me.

I retreated to the ladies' room. I'd kiss a mule's ass before I let him see me cry. That was the first time I'd heard the Voice. It said: "Hundreds of centuries we have been. For centuries, we will be. We look upon no face but our own."

I sat still; I held my breath. I looked around for someone, knowing I had locked the door.

The Voice spoke again. "Never bow your head to anyone except in respect. Experience is a gift; accept it gratefully. Treat it as a friend you love from a distance."

Three months later, I was offered another job in another city with a satisfying promotion as a counselor. That suited me just fine. I got a doctorate in Psychology and became a corporate advisor specializing in stress management.

As Ted alluded, the sisters protected me, guided me. They were like the voice in our heads that tell us, 'Don't do that,' or 'Call your mother'. If we follow the advice, we feel good; trouble usually followed if we don't.

But my Voices were more than that. I sensed their perpetuity. Theirs was not power one should idolize fear. It just was. They were loving, merciful, kind. It made me leave Columbus, and guided me home today. I named them SUKU – Seen Unseen-Known Unknown. They had said it would do.

Grandmother tried to move, and winced in pain from the effort. Again, Ted read my mind. "I am not here to hurt your grandmother. I can't; it is not within us. But, unfortunately, our presence can cause the living to hurt themselves. That is not my purpose either. I have been with MaeAlice a long time now. Not every minute, but then time has no meaning in reality. I last visited when your daughter was born."

My eyes widened. "What? Why?"

"MaeAlice couldn't see me then, but Shannon could. We had a very interesting chat that day. Babies can see things clearly, you know. We made a bargain, Grace, Shannon and I, in the months before she was born."

"What are you talking about?"

"You must listen, Grace. When I'm done, you have a decision to make. And trust me, it is one of life and death. One MaeAlice made, your mother made, and now you have to make. You have seen how the simplest decision can have disturbing and lasting effects. Every event influences the next event, Grace, just like every second is connected to a minute and every minute to an hour, and then days and months to years."

Even in the midst of anxiety, I was struck by how properly Ted spoke. Almost sophisticated. I leaned back in my chair, finding a place to rest my head. Despite my feelings about him, I sensed Ted was about to share something no other visitor had. Despite his claim, he had information I desperately sought.

Ted continued. "I made a simple decision to leave Baltimore. Every day thereafter, I made choices. Not always good ones, I'm afraid. But starting over in Blessing didn't stop the consequences of decisions I had made before. You need to know about one of those choices in order to understand everything that followed, even up to MaeAlice lying here between us."

Ted sat down at Grandmother's feet. I thought that odd since he had no body in the physical sense. Nonetheless, I could see him: hands, feet, even shoes. Satisfied with the position, he began his story.

Chapter 24: *Ted*

"Baltimore was a sleepy little town then. Not much to do there, especially for a man like myself. You've traveled there. You know what I'm talking about. One day, my best friend stopped by my salon. I was a hairdresser. Can you believe that? Processed men's hair in the back room of a beauty parlor.

"My customers used the back door; they wouldn't be seen going into a beauty shop. That's where I learned the art of seducing women. That beauty parlor. The women I worked with told me all about the things a woman want from a man. Good teachers, every one. And I learned.

"Anyway, Lawrence pops in and whispers in my ear. There was no privacy in the salon. Every word spoken in that place ended up in someone else's conversation as soon as it left your mouth. What he told me got me excited in one part of my brain and scared out of the other. I had a customer halfway through a konk. I washed him out and told him to come back tomorrow. He fussed, but I closed the shop and left with Lawrence.

"Lawrence was a gigolo. He wasn't that much to look at, your average guy, but he had *something* and women were willing to pay for it. He had been trying to hook me up for more than a year, but I couldn't get with that at the time. He understood my hesitation. We grew up together. Lived on the same street. Believe it or not, we grew up in the church. I believed that business about sin; Lawrence didn't. But he respected that I did.

"The woman he was working at the time was loaded. Husband had died in a plane crash. Had insurance everywhere that paid double indemnity on top of the airline settlement. No children. Lawrence persuaded her to marry him two months after the man was buried. He still hustled his other women behind her back. Guess he couldn't give it up. Besides, it paid well and Lawrence liked money. With all he had, he wanted more.

"About four months into the marriage, she found him cheating. Told her it was because he didn't want to ask her for change, all the while spending her money like he'd worked forty hours to earn it. She told him she'd make him beneficiary of everything and give him access to one of her bank accounts if he gave up the other women. If she caught him cheating again, he'd lose everything. He agreed. She followed through. Put his name on everything up front to show she meant it.

"But Lawrence couldn't keep his promise. He was much younger than she and still had the scent of women in his nose. She caught him, in her own house. Headed straight for her attorney but she never got to his office. Her car was stolen with her in it. 'Killed in the commission of a crime' That's what the police report said. Luckily for Lawrence, she hadn't called her lawyer so they had nothing except speculation. He got everything. That's what he whispered in my ear, he was rich; the first check had come. All total, he was expecting millions.

"My cut was three hundred thousand dollars for helping him. I could barely say it much less imagine that kind of money. That was my share. The carjacker was never caught. He ended up in Blessing with over a quarter-million dollars. Funny, don't you think; how I could kill a woman for money but couldn't sleep with one for it.

"So, I moved to Blessing. I was afraid to stay in Baltimore and start spending money everyone knew I didn't have. That's how I met your grandmother. By helping Lawrence, I stepped into his world. When I got here, I decided to live like he did. Except, I still didn't sleep with women for money, I just used them for what I needed. I used MaeAlice and Eva Lee. I used Janette who hid me after... Daniel...

"Grace, you have no reason to believe me but I hated the way Mae treated you and those kids. I told her many times to ease up. She told me just as many that her family was none of my business. When I first met your grandmother, I went to her trying to help. I thought giving her money would make it right. Eventually, I stopped trying. I know I took a lot of my anger out on Daniel but I never meant to kill him.

"MaeAlice was a hard woman, Grace. Something soured her heart long before me. After passing over I learned what it was. I also discovered my coming to Blessing had meaning. Still, after MaeAlice took me in I made other choices that failed her."

I wondered where all this was going. Why had he chosen Grandmother, of all the women in Blessing? And because he did, what did it have to do with me, now? What did it have to do with Shannon?

"It will come clear Grace, I promise," he said, and paused. "It was meant that Daniel die. It was ordained before Daniel was born."

"What the hell are you talking about? You had no choice but to kill him? Is that what you're saying!"

"I'm saying choices have consequences. All of them."

Chapter 25: *Disclosure*

Questions erupted inside my head. He said this involved my daughter. Shannon was the first-born female of the first-born female like generations of first-born women before her. Why wouldn't she be involved? Besides, I had summoned her to Blessing.

Ted added, "You're here today, Grace, because it's time you learn of a decision you must make. Before you make it, you have to know the truth. Only MaeAlice can tell you that. Let's just say I'm here for moral support."

"A decision about what?"

"About an unborn child."

"Don't talk to me in riddles!"

"I'm talking about the son you lost. And the grandson yet to be born."

Ted let that statement linger. Fog invaded my brain. He had to know I needed answers but he changed the subject.

"Do you remember the old man who helped MaeAlice kill hogs? He told you some very important facts about being in the living experience. Do you remember any of what he said?"

"Yes, I remember almost everything he said. Not the exact words. He said all life has value; that everything is here to serve. That it's more harmful to do something grudgingly than to not do it at all."

Ted responded. "When I was in the living experience, I believed in sin, went to church often, and yet never gave God, as some call it, much thought. But everything we do, to help or hurt someone becomes a ripple in time, like a stone dropped in water. And every wave will touch the lives of people you'll never meet. Think about that Grace, the good you do reaches across time and affects someone you'll never know."

"And so do the things that hurt. Right?" I heard him and wanted him to hear me. "Those things not only cross time, they cross the boundaries of life, don't they, Ted?" The tone in my voice surprised me. The words tasted thick, like blue-black ink; hot, like Sahara sand. Instantly, I remembered the woman at the tombstone I had seen as a child. Realization. "She's followed you across time hasn't she; the woman you killed."

"Yes, but we are talking about you, Shannon, and MaeAlice—all rings in a bigger tree." Ted let his point linger. "The old man told you that a thing whose soul is not free gets trapped. Well, the soul can be trapped for many reasons. The two things most often at the root of entrapment are anger and guilt. That was true for the woman you saw. She has both. Much of it attributed to Lawrence. There is tremendous passion over what he did to her. And she feels sorrow because she knew what kind of man he was and ignored it, tried to buy her way through it. Like every one of us, she shares responsibility for what happened to her. She made decisions in the same way Lawrence made decisions."

Ted shifted on the bed, which, again, seemed an odd thing to do. "Her name was Shelia Paxon. Something I did hundreds of miles away came to your doorstep. It's all connected, Grace. That's why she led you to that tombstone. Although you are strongly empathetic, what you're feeling now is not her anger but your own."

"What do you know about my anger?" I felt the heat from the words on my teeth. This man killed what my grandmother loved.

As if he heard my thought, he said, "I regret your grandmother suffered, but it could not be helped. Things are not what they seem. Sometimes help comes as a dearest friend riding on the back of pain. And sometimes decisions, once made, can not be taken back; can't be fixed."

His words pounded my heart. A chill hit my face and stung like needles of ice. "I gotta go." I said out loud. "You've been torturing this woman for thirty years and you say you're here to help her!? Help her to where, you son-of-a-bitch; to where?"

"You were there, Grace. You've seen what anger is capable of. You must heal your own, or Shannon will pay as you do now. Ripples across time, remember?"

"So that's why you're here—spinning bullshit about an unborn child and ethereal agreements with Shannon for revenge? What did I ever do to you?" I was on my feet with my hand on the door when Ted stopped me.

"Don't you want to know what happened to the money?"

He said he had brought three hundred thousand dollars with him. He tried giving Grandmother a few bills when he first met her, but had not bought so much as a car.

"I see you still like mysteries. I was counting on that. But right now, yes, you should go. Olivia needs you."

Chapter 26: *Returning Home*

The path to Grandmother's old house had overgrown with weeds. Hers was the first built on the street they'd later name Tate. No one knew why; no Tates ever lived there.

Some thought is was the name of some dead white family the town council assigned to reign over the black folk who settled here. To the rest of us, it was 'Around the Corner' because it was about a mile walk from the town that had no traffic light. Its library shared space with the ice cream store. There was not room enough for either.

Nola built her house twelve years ago in the same neighborhood. She and Jim helped to clear the spot but built from scratch differently than Grandmother had done; they used contractors. Not one had a license, but their skill was sought by those who did. Grandmother had had but a few men of varied ages, an old mule, a few sticks of dynamite, and her ax.

Tiny sweet gum trees reached their limbs across the old path as if playing a game of tag. Grandmother had used their sprigs as a toothbrush that stayed in her mouth all day. She'd said the fibers were sweet. I broke a sprig, peeled back the bark, and stuck it in my mouth. As the first moisture found taste buds, I spat. Perhaps it was a different kind of tree. Still, I let the twig stay and calmed myself with the smell of honeysuckle that sprayed from everywhere.

As I rounded the turn in the path I saw Olivia at the kitchen door. She was tossing a pail of water in the direction of two old dogs that had heard the door swing open. They expected scraps of food like always. They were surprised to see water headed their way, and made a yelping escape. Olivia looked up to see me making my way through the brush.

Quickly, she met me at the corner of the old clothesline. The poles' outstretched arms once stood straight; once held a parade of garments that twisted and turned as they dried in a mixture of gentle breezes and bright summer sun. Now they leaned, the stiffness in their limb decayed with time. I hoped the stiffness in Olivia's attitude for Grandmother had shared the same decay.

In perfect symmetry, we placed ourselves into each other's arms. In thirty-one years, our love for each other had survived. Dormant until this moment, it all came back. This was the purity of our bond and the unspoken promise solidified long ago.

"Look at you! Who knew all this was hiding in that skinny little girl whose best friend was a book." She turned me as if a dance and said, " Come on, help me finish. We'll sit outside like old times and you can tell me everything."

Without notice, she pulled me towards the steps that had conveyed us in the ups and downs, the ins and outs of this little house for so many years. We were young again.

I rinsed my hands in the kitchen sink and set about tearing lettuce and slicing tomatoes. Outside, Olivia spread a dark pink tablecloth with colored butterflies. The little creatures looked to have just landed, here and there, to rest. She'd filled the tray with a pitcher of lemonade, cloth napkins, silverware, and the 'good' china that Grandmother never used. The dishes had always sat so pretty in the cabinet, one plate upon another so fragile the magnolia petals might bruise if we touched them.

"You're using these?"

"And what do you think plates are for? I'd bet these things haven't been out of that cabinet since she set them in there forty years ago. I had to soak them for twenty minutes just to find their color. She was always saving things for special occasions. I'd say this qualifies, don't you?"

Olivia stood still for a moment, letting her eyes take in all of me. "I haven't seen my best friend in over thirty years; she's grown into a beautiful woman, a successful professional, so I hear, with a beautiful daughter—no doubt—and the old woman is dying. What better reasons to celebrate?"

The dinner, the special china, was for me. My arms reached for her and held on tightly. Unlike the reunion embrace moments ago, this one held forgiveness. The anger I'd held over her leaving dripped like melting ice. It was the warmth in Olivia's arms, the sanctity of her love that saved me.

"Come on, lets go catch up." She led me to a feast of cold foods arrayed on the table accented with butterflies. Chilled lemon slices floated in their own hazy liquid inside sparkling glasses.

The torridness I had fought coming home was relenting for the day. Olivia and I bowed our heads in silent thanksgiving. A maiden breeze touched the cloth, lifting the butterflies.

"Aunt Liv, it's too pretty to eat."

"No such thing. Grab that big fork there."

I obeyed. Putting the matching colored napkin on my lap, I wondered where Olivia had found all the lovely things. Grandmother had never set a table anywhere near this. In fact, Grandmother had never set a table at all. I had to ask.

"I found it all in an old trunk of stuff the other day," Olivia said. Rinsing was all they needed. I hung them on the clothesline to dry, rickety as it was, it held up. Didn't even have to iron them."

"I never knew Granny had such beautiful things," I confessed.

"Girl, there are two trunks of stuff like this in there. Clothes with tags still on 'em. Stuff never opened. Some of it has to be collector's items by now."

We ate quietly, reverently; each forkful filled the hunger of thirty years of my needing her company. The sun had nearly closed its eyes for the day. Streaks of mango and lavender played across the sky like kites on a string. I remembered us sharing a day with the same sovereignty so many times before. Finally, I began the journey on which I had been sent. I began, not for Grandmother's sake, but my own.

"Why didn't you ever write?"

"Well, that puts it on the table doesn't it," Olivia said. "I knew it would come up but didn't think it would be the opening bell." She put her fork down and bowed her head. A heavy sigh fanned her chest.

I picked at my salad. I placed a broken saltine in my mouth to make sure I didn't speak again. Olivia did not respond immediately.

"Grace. I was wrong. I should have been in touch with you all these years. I looked for you to say good bye." She stopped and started again. "That's not entirely true, I wanted to take you with me. You may not remember but Nola and you kids stayed with me before she went to New York. She left you with Momma because she said I was still wild, and didn't need to add three kids to the one I already had. I believe that began our fighting, even though she was right. As for taking you with me, Momma never would have let me. Besides, Lyn and Dillon needed you. I looked for you. I knew you were out there," she said, turning her head towards the tombstones, "but you didn't answer."

"That doesn't answer my question," I said. Words that covered the question without answering it always annoyed me, even now. Evasive maneuvers. With my clients, I'd simply repeat the question.

"No, it doesn't," Olivia replied. She hesitated, filled her mouth again and chewed. She did this as if the mixture on her fork would transform into the answer I needed. "Perhaps if I tell you how I came to leave, you will understand why I never wrote."

This was not the focus of my question, but I was about to get an answer I waited years to hear—what had gone wrong between Olivia and Grandmother. I set my fork down; nothing would distract me. Not the crunch of a cucumber or the vinegary flavor of pickled okra.

Olivia pushed back her chair. She picked up the serving plate and the pitcher of lemonade and headed towards the house. I didn't move; the question I'd asked play in my head, waiting for closure.

Olivia returned with a bottle of champagne and two long stem glasses. The final glint of day was nearly gone. That hazy dusk announcing the soon arrival of fireflies settled in.

"Nola called just now. Said Shannon is there. I asked for thirty minutes before she comes up." She then popped the cork and poured from the black glass bottle. Suds floated to the top of the delicate, crystal glasses. It sizzled loud enough to hear.

"Champagne?"

"I'm assuming you've learned to drink by now. And if you haven't, this is a liquid worthy of your inauguration. Besides, I'm home. Celebrating. You're here, sharing it with me and that makes it all the sweeter." Olivia picked up her glass and tilted it in my direction. She smiled, then, sipped. Shortly, she began.

"It was the night before Daniel was buried. The Wake. Your mother and I had fought over everything all day long, all of which was nothing. You and I had talked over there, in that bedroom for the dead. You were confused about having Nola back; I worked on how to tell Momma what happened to Daniel. The wake was over; everyone was gone. I had to tell her how my brother died. I knew how she'd react. I even thought about letting Slang tell her. Do you remember him?" she asked. "Wow, I hadn't thought about him until now." She brushed the thought aside.

"Anyway, it was my duty to tell her, not his. I went to her room. She was already drowsy from the medication; I hoped it would help her hear what I had to say. Giving her that news was difficult, Grace, because Momma and I never got along, not from the day I was big enough to walk. That happens sometimes between mothers and daughters. It's like I was born with a grudge against her. In my case, I think she hated me because I was born.

"I learned, after moving to New York, that while she was pregnant with me, Papa started beating on her. She would push her stomach out at him to take the blows, hoping he would stop for fear of hurting me, I suppose. Once, he cut her with a knife, just a prick because the knife was dull but she bled as if it had been a razor. That may be when I began my hate for her.

"Maybe she was angry with me for holding on and not dying in her womb. When I was old enough, she beat me, for every reason she could find and sometimes for no reason at all. All my time in this house was lived in conflict with her.

"Later, Daniel was born and became what she loved. I think she and Papa still fought early on. Then Papa was gone; I never saw him again. When I went to her room that night to tell her why her son was dead, a part of me wanted to be the one to tell her."

Olivia changed mid-stream again. "Was there talk about how Daniel died after I left?"

"People said Ted killed him. But he was never found." I did not tell her that I had spoken with him an hour ago.

"The story was no rumor. The man your grandmother took into her bed killed what she loved most. That is what I told her." Olivia stopped there. She got up and walked to the nearest tree, turning her back to me, bracing against its trunk. "Grace, have you ever had someone you love tell you they hated the air that comes from your lungs? That God should curse the earth beneath your feet?"

She didn't expect an answer because she kept talking. "Momma didn't want to hear the truth. She called me a bitch and said I was like all the other whores who wanted Ted. 'Bringing me lies,' is what she said. I knew she was hurting and the medicine had her out of her mind; saying things she might not have said. But then, I remembered how much she hates me and I knew those words were hers. I pulled her up by her arms and shook her. When I realized what I was doing, I let her go. She fell back to the pillow. A voice came out of her that was so reeked in hatred I could smell it on her breath. Her eyes went cold. She said I was like my daddy.

"I knew what that meant. The first time Papa hit her she was two months pregnant with me. She hadn't done dinner. In all the time they were married, she always had dinner on the table when he came home. I guess that day he'd had more than he could take from the man who controlled his livelihood. All he wanted was to eat and sleep. But she had been sick all day because of me. Uncle Book told me this on the drive to New York. Lots of highway and he knew I was hurting.

"That night, she said, 'You've been nothing but pain to me from the day you was conceived'. That I was an offense that God should pluck from her sight."

Olivia walked back to her chair. She sat gingerly as if the weight of her next words were too heavy on which to stand. "Grace, my mother told me that I should have died in her womb. There was something about her eyes. Through all her meanness, I had never seen that look. She said, 'why won't *you* die? Why wasn't it you instead?' Imagine, Grace, the feeling you had thinking your mother abandoned you? Add the notion that she never wanted you in the first place. That will help you begin to know how I felt that night."

Night sat in Olivia's heart; her shoulders sagged forward. "A letter to you would have been the same as her touching me. I couldn't do it. I know you know what I'm talking about Grace. I know you know."

Chapter 27: *Shannon*

Shannon arrived at the house on Tate Street in time to see Olivia and me holding hands across the table. Instead of the path, she walked the paved shoulder of the highway with a couple of kids in tow. I put my arms around my daughter. "As always, perfect timing."

"Here, let me look at you," Olivia requested, playfully pulling me away from the woman-child. Shannon stood back. The long black mane she'd inherited from Nola spilled from the loop in the back of her baseball cap. Wearing it was habit. She rarely primped and it was perfect for the lab.

The sun had been gone for almost an hour but remnants of day remained. Olivia lifted the cap from Shannon's face to see joy shape almond eyes and embarrassment curl softly colored lips.

"Oh, Grace. She's beautiful." Olivia said. Shannon lowered her head, hiding the sting in her cheeks. She'd heard this word applied to her many times, and she'd learned to ignore it. But there was sincerity in Olivia's voice that made her blush; made her believe it was true.

"Come, sit down," Olivia told Shannon, as she shooed the escorts back to Nola's with her free hand. The children raced each other down the tar and graveled artery. "Your mother said you're studying to be a doctor. You'll be the first in our family."

"I start residency next year, if I'm lucky."

"Luck? Child, luck ain't a condition this family requires. I know your mother. She's as smart as Solomon so you have to have gotten some of that. But residency is rough. How will you manage with a baby?"

"We'll work that out," I assured Olivia.

"Little Wren's father will be back by then. He's military," Shannon added. "We had a simple ceremony before he left but didn't know I was pregnant till after. Shannon rubbed her belly. "Needless to say, this came as a surprise to all of us."

Satisfied, Olivia changed the subject. She looked directly at me and asked, "I know what your gift is; what can this young lady do?"

Shannon's lips parted in surprise. Unlike the women before me, I helped Shannon to manage and appreciate her talents. She also knew I never talked about it to anyone else. To hear Olivia speak of it with such certainty caught her off guard.

78

"How do you know about mom?" Shannon asked.

"Baby girl, I was there when your mother first learned she was different. Your great-grand mother tried to beat it out of her; deep down I think MaeAlice knew, too, but she'd never admit it. She didn't even admit her own. You know how good she was with dirt. Could put one seed in the ground and get back three bushels of whatever it was. That was her gift. She always gave God the credit, which was right to do, I reckon."

Shannon's curious stare went to Olivia, then to me.

Olivia paid her surprise no mind and kept on talking.

"The first time I knew your momma had it was when she told me about seeing my brother almost to the minute he died." She turned to me, "Did you tell her about that?" but didn't wait for the answer. "That's when I knew. Then she'd go to that graveyard over there all the time," nodding her head at the time-beaten tombstones leaning from old neglect. "I knew she was out there talking to the residents. After that, I always wondered who else she saw and what they had to say. I left shortly after that so never had a chance to find out."

Olivia stopped to breathe, still staring at the fungus-layered granite shapes, as if she could see what I had seen. I knew she was reliving the event that took her brother. That event severed what love she'd held onto for her mother, and forced her away from me. The scab on thirty years of hurt covered wounds that had not healed.

Shannon touched her great aunt's arm. The sadness flowing through Olivia's veins was thick as mud and just as gritty. I knew because I had felt the same pallid hue in Grandmother over the years. It was the color of happiness gone bad—deprived, drained and forgotten.

Olivia lifted Shannon's fingers from her arm and patted her hand. "Oh, goodness; dark has sneaked up on us. It's too nice to go inside. Let me get one of those old kerosene lamps. Believe it or not, I found one while going through stuff in the old woman's closet. Even found a can of oil in the pantry. Both might still work." Olivia forced a smile, pushed her chair away from the table, and walked quickly to the house.

Shannon looked at me. "She's a very sad woman, mom. What happened?"

"The same thing that happened to Grandma. Love died between them."

Olivia pushed open the screen door carrying a glass lantern in one hand and a bottle of oil in the other. She sat both down and prepared to make magic. She winked as blue heat danced beneath a yellow burst of light. "Oh, that's nice," she said, and sat the globe in place. "So, young lady," she continued, looking at me. "What have you seen lately?"

I laughed guardedly. "Are you sure you don't have a gift of your own?"

"Well then, tell me!" Olivia encouraged. "I always loved your stories. Haven't had one in a long, long time. Come on, Spill it."

I wasn't ready to tell Aunt Liv about Ted. "I'm gonna get some more of that melon. Shannon, you have to try it. I'll bring back the bowl and some saucers." Like Olivia, I all but ran towards the house. When I returned, Shannon and Olivia were laughing. Olivia had told one of her jokes—probably a dirty one. She hadn't lost her sense of humor. I placed a bowl in front of each woman. The chocolate had hardened in the refrigerator and the melon cooled, just enough. Shannon oohed at the pleasure contained in chocolate and honeydew, chocolate and strawberries, and just chocolate.

Olivia turned to Shannon. "How was MaeAlice when you left?"

Shannon saw what I meant. "She was okay. Still seeing things," Shannon said.

"My guess is her evil ass is seeing the people she did wrong. They must be yanking her toes."

Everyone had told Shannon about the hatred Olivia had for her mother but seeing first-hand gave it life. "Aunt Liv, do you really want Grandma to die?" I asked.

"Don't matter to me one way or the other."

"What if it does matter? Grandma is almost done with this life. She's moving on soon. And you have a chance to make peace between the two of you. What if that matters?"

"Peace?" Olivia shouted. "The only peace I want is to know she's dead."

"You don't mean that; I know you don't, otherwise you wouldn't be here."

"I told her I'd come home when she was in a pine box. That shouldn't be long. I hope she'll be looking at my face when she takes her last breath."

"Grandma has been dying a painful slow death for a long time. It didn't start with you Aunt Liv, and it didn't start the day Uncle Daniel died."

"Yeah, I know. It started the day I was conceived," Olivia replied.

"Here's a story for you, Aunt Liv. You don't know this, but after you left, I had a really bad accident. We'd come home from church and I was putting away our clothes. I stepped onto the cedar chest in the closet to hang up my dress. I lost balance and fell into a pot of water on the kerosene heater. Burned myself so bad..."

The memory made me hold my breath, as if not breathing kept me safe. "They called a fire talker. She said she was too old to hold the fire and Grandma had to do it. Before she did, she told Grandma, 'Everything seeks its own'."

Shannon was also hearing this story for the first time. Both women sat still, listening. They knew this was more than just recounting Grandmother's life. Neither would miss a word, to do so was to miss a piece of the mystery that was Grandmother. And a piece of me.

"The old woman talked the fire from my body. She said it purified me. But something different happened to Grandma. She was always cold after that. She needed a fire around her all the time. She wore sweaters in the summer. You couldn't go into her room because heat would suck the oxygen right out of your lungs. Saving me cost her; in a big way, but she and I became closer.

"When I fell onto that pot of water, it was because I saw someone. The same person Grandma sees now. Ted."

"Wait a minute," Olivia interrupted. How did he get in your room?" She shook her head in denial. "No, he was gone. Nobody knows what happened to Ted or where he went. You couldn't have seen him."

"It was Ted, Aunt Liv. He told me earlier today why he was there that day and why he visits Grandma now."

"So you're telling me that bastard killed my brother, and has been haunting my mother all these years. That he caused you to fall! That means he's been dead all this time. How?"

"Ted died the same night you left. He told me he'd been chosen to help grandma when he was alive but didn't. He wants you to know it was not his will to kill

82

Daniel and that he's deeply sorry for his part in causing you to leave."

Agitated, Olivia asked, "Is he here now? If you can hear me motherfucker, I hope you're burning in the hell you created for the rest of us. I'm glad you're dead, you son-of-a bitch!" Her hands gripped the metal armrests of the patio chair. She flung her head from side to side, as if expecting him to step from behind the big oak tree.

Shannon began to understand. The thing between Olivia and her great-grandmother had spun into hate around the man called Ted. The sadness she felt in Olivia's body was gestating long before Ted, but he had set it loose. Shannon spoke for the first time since I had begun this tale. "Mom, we need to talk."

"That's a good idea," Olivia chimed. "You two talk." Her voice had settled an octave lower but her eyes smoldered. She walked quickly up the driveway to the little stretch of highway that zigzagged towards Nola's. She walked in the opposite direction.

The flame in the oil lamp flickered wildly and returned to a steady glow. Shannon repositioned her pregnant weight in the patio chair. "Mom, talk to me. I had a strong sensation when you called this man's name. He must be what I felt in Grandma's room. Why is he here; what does he want?"

"I don't know what Ted's motive is, sweetheart. The story he told me felt true; that he wants to help. That's all I can tell."

I took a deep breath. "He told me that he knows you; that he saw you come into the world; that you made him some kind of promise. He also told me that Grandma only has a short time left and she has to tell us something."

"What promise?"

"I don't know," I said. "The answers are in Grandmother's room." Shannon nodded her agreement. I reached for the lamp and turned out the fire. Night draped itself comfortably upon everything around us. Holding onto my daughter's hand, I led us down the dimly lit highway. Back to Grandmother, back to Ted.

Chapter 28: *Facing Ted*

Except for the low sounds of a TV, the house was quiet when Shannon and I arrived. It was almost ten o'clock. We made our way down the hall covered in mass produced prints depicting black life in America. A child sitting at the feet of an old man playing a guitar. Two little girls playing patty-cake. A baptism in a country pond surrounded by more bush than onlookers. Dillon had been a fabulous photographer; Nola had pieces of his original work, but hung these instead. His prints should have hung in art galleries and likely would had he lived longer.

In Grandmother's room, a tiny lamp did its best to make shadows. The strain of its effort was enough to show that Ted was waiting.

"You've grown into a beautiful woman, like your mother," he said. "Both of you please, sit. You have questions."

Neither of us expressed surprise; we expected him there. Shannon sat on the twin bed the nurse used when she slept over. "What is this about?"

"Your son."

Shannon looked at me; I looked at Ted. Everyone naturally assumed it was a girl since all the women as far back as we could trace had delivered first-born daughters.

It was a fact as sure as the sun rising each day. But only she and I knew for sure that it was a boy.

"What the hell are you talking about?" Shannon said, louder than she expected.

"Ask your grandmother."

I turned my attention to her. "Granny?"

My eyes had adjusted to the dim light enough to see that she was crying. She clutched the covers. Her lips trembled.

Ted said, "I will start for her." He moved towards Grandmother. "The first-born women in your family made a vow long before time had meaning. They accepted an arrangement that allows them to develop and pass special powers across their lineage, strengthening that power with each generation."

"For what purpose?" I asked.

"One of your lineage will change life as you know it. She will create something new out of a life that she must take. By doing so, she will save it. "

Shannon was incredulous. "You mean all this cloak and dagger, is about saving someone's life?"

"That life is important. It is a new creature and will change everything."

"Every life is important," I said.

"Yes, we all have a mission in the scheme of things. But the life we're talking about will be called the face of God."

"People hear that every Sunday," I said.

Shannon had moved on. "You know who this person is?" She asked.

"Yes."

I remembered what started this and put the question back to Ted. "What has Shannon's son to do with this?"

"That person is her son."

"Are you messing with our heads? What is going on?" I asked, far too loudly.

Ted looked at Grandmother.

Like a candle slowly weeps its life away, drop-by-drop, she spoke the secret. "Your son must die."

"Both of you are crazy," I said. "How can you say such a horrible thing?"

"My son was sacrificed, Grace. So was Dillon, so was your son, as was every first-born male child before them."

She was right. Dillon was the first boy born to Nola; Daniel was grandmother's only son. Both were dead. "Those were accidents!" I said. "Horrible accidents."

"And your son, Grace, what was he?"

"He was never born, I miscarried."

"The blood of your first sons is the payments for what you are," Ted said. "It doesn't matter if they are conceived first, last or in the middle. To die unborn was a gift."

Grandmother added, "We never know how long we have them if they are born; they don't tell us that, but none has ever reached manhood. Each mother must choose for her great grandchild."

"What!"

"Mom, she's saying my brother's death was on purpose," Shannon said.

"She's also saying she decided the death of your child." I turned to Grandmother. "Are both of you crazy? And what do you mean, gift? Killing my child was a gift? Are both of you crazy?"

"Grandma Alice decided my child dies?"

"No, baby, she didn't."

"Grace," Ted said, "All of us are given the choice of how we contribute to life. The ancient ones know making

86

such a decision is a burden no person should live with. So, moments after birth, while we still see angels and talk to spirits, the ancient ones ask us to decide. It's within those moments that every child is shown his or her mission and with the wisdom of ages, we all accept or decline to carry forth our intention and thereby put in motion the ripples across time.

"Your clan accepted what appears to be an horrific experience. And, so, at the birth of each grandchild, the grandmother is revisited to decide the next generation."

"You're saying that my son died for this; that my grandson and great grandson will die. For what!"

"Only a girl-child can pass through our bodies first," Grandmother said.

The weight of her words exploded in my head. Shannon's mouth began to tremble. "My son will not be born?" she managed to say.

"Your lineage is that of sages. Within your DNA are the secrets of God." Ted added. "You know without knowing. For the greater humanity, yes, you have given the lives of your sons, and your sons have accepted their fate. But this child has to live for that to happen."

Shannon spoke with hope. "And what has this to do with you? Are you here to help us save him? Was that the agreement we made?"

"No, Shannon. I'm here to see that he dies."

Chapter 29: *SuKu – The Secret*

The MaeAlice giggled. She retreated from Ted's words and drifted to a time in which she had control, to the time she made things grow.

The MaeAlice began tilling the plot of dirt she owned right after her house was built. Alongside the men who helped, she dug up tree stumps and roots buried deep as her misery. She walked the old brown mule behind the plow her father had used. Sunshine had kissed this earth for thousands of years just as it did today. The soil she plowed was black as night. It smelled sweet, like the core of a peach. MaeAlice loved this earth. She'd stoop sometimes, pick up a handful and suck the fragrance through her nostrils. Its vapors filled her head. Sometimes she'd taste it—clay deep from the soul of its mother. Sometimes, she crumbled it, exposing rocks and arrows, broken pieces of someone else's life. Late in the evening, she'd dig a hole on the edge of her land, in a spot not likely to be disturbed, and place the pieces there.

The MaeAlice knew the earth; the earth knew her, her hands knew something her brain would never understand. The earth, and they, participated in an unspoken agreement made before her birth. Because of this agreement, the St.John household was never hungry. The icebox, kept in a back room, was always full of frozen beneficence from the patch of land she tended. During the summer, she'd set up a small stand on the side of the road just outside the town that had no stoplight. The children helped sell vegetables to passersby.

Many of the white patrons became regulars, stopping by every week for the twelve weeks of the St. John market.

They made conversation and began calling MaeAlice by her first name as if their shiny coins bought them that right. They wanted her secrets, thinking they'd paid for the privilege to ask. She was a St.John. Her husband had come from Trinidad. Certainly, there had to be some secret mixture she sprinkled in her rows to grow such copious crops.

But MaeAlice never told. Sometimes she'd smile and say, "The Lord's been good. No telling what I'll get next year. I'm just glad this year's been a blessing." Other times she'd say, "A good crop starts with good seed. What's in the seed is bound to come out." Perhaps that's all there was to it. Maybe there was nothing more to tell. What was in the seed was bound to come out.

The Mr. Jim asked her to grow on the land he owned not far from her house. He promised to split the profits. Trees, brush and bigotry separated their land. He was a white man whose family owned most of Blessing. The ten acres he handed her to tend had grown tobacco and cotton, the source of his legacy. MaeAlice had worked for him in those fields. Picked, suckled, primed and cropped everything he grew. She knew his land.

"Not much grow there now, I 'pect," she said. "Ground done give what it could. Too much been took from it over the years. You gotta give something back. Take a while to turn it 'round'."

"Go to the general store; my brother will give whatever you need. I got some field hands I can spare. Tell them what to do; they won't give you no trouble."

The following year, quarter-mile rows spilled with sweet potatoes, corn, peas, beans, cantaloupe, squash, onions, white potatoes, and tomatoes on Mr. Jim's land. MaeAlice entrusted her garden to the children; it was theirs to tend, though she kept a watchful eye.

At the start of the third year of his agreement, Mr. Jim took back his land. Business had been too good to continue splitting the profits; she was living better than she should, by his standards.

One of the field hands Mr. Jim had assigned with his agreement told MaeAlice what he'd said. The hand ended his telling by saying, "He ain't learnt yet that it take more than a plow and cow chips to do what you did."

Someone else was in charge of Mr. Jim's land now, but MaeAlice stayed on to work, family necessity dictated. When asked how she felt about what Mr. Jim had done, she replied, "Suit me just fine if it never rain another drop on that piece of dirt. Suit me just fine." She resigned her concern to the patch of dirt that fed her family year round.

It wasn't long before The Mr. Jim came knocking on her door. MaeAlice entertained her customers with the story. "Yeah, he come back. Had some dirt in his hand. Asked me if I could tell him what it needed. Poor dirt. I could almost hear it crying. They done burnt it to death with them chemicals. Thought he knew better. Humpf."

The patrons egged her on, chuckling at her telling of the day she turned Mr. Jim away from her door with dirt seeping through his fingers.

"What'd you tell him, Ms. Mae," they asked.

"I told him it needed a friend." Everyone slapped their knees and choked on laughter.

Those days were good for MaeAlice. The glass was worn harmless and the cinders were cool in this patch of her journey. It was also on this stretch of life that The Mae-Alice began her descent into the hell everyone condemned her. It was in this patch some say the devil came for his due.

Chapter 30: *Run*

"Grab your bag, we're leaving."

Shannon had already come to the same conclusion and was reaching for her purse as the words came from my mouth. I looked at the clock to calculate the drive to Virginia. I turned my attention to Ted. "No one, not you, not God, is harming this child. You hear me!"

Ted didn't respond. That angered me as much as his speech. We drove in silence for the first hour, each of us processing what we heard in our own way. The Virginia state line sign came into view as if it meant safety. I actually heard Shannon relax.

"Are you okay, baby?"

"Yes, mom." A nervous laugh followed. "When you said come to Blessing, this was not what I expected. But I'm good."

Shannon shifted her weight. A McDonald's was up ahead. Locked in tension since we'd left, we stopped for a restroom break. I needed something cool and decided on a milkshake and fries.

"Same for me," Shannon called back on her way to the restroom. "And chicken nuggets with mustard."

We sat in the restaurant and ate. Outside, two guys were in a heated conversation; each was pressed hard against the car door where he sat. Shortly, Shannon and I broached the subject from which we were fleeing.

"Dean really wants this baby, Mom. I can't imagine my life without it." She looked down at her eight months of wonder.

"You won't have to," I said, even knowing I couldn't guarantee his life. History called me a liar and fear mocked my words. Daniel was dead. Dillon was dead. My son was never born. The same fate was decided for Shannon's child, and I had no idea how to stop it.

We finished the meal and headed for the door. The car with the two guys was still there but the argument had intensified. Shannon and I walked past. From the corner of my eye, I saw Ted sitting in the backseat of the friction. My mind froze just as a noise pierced the air. Time must have slowed because a frightening silence occupied the space between the sound of gunshot and the scream.

Chapter 31: *Fate*

The ambulance raced towards Richmond. Paramedics did their best to stop the bleeding. Shannon's pulse was weak and the baby's weaker. They talked in measured tones on the radio about the shooting victim and the eight-month fetus whose vitals were indecipherable. I held my daughter's hand and felt her essence dim, her breath given by a machine. I could sense Wren passing on but the attendants would not pronounce him.

When we arrived at the hospital, several nurses and a doctor were waiting at the entrance. Immediately, they began efforts to save my daughter and spare her son from death. One pulled me aside and gathered information her form said she needed to help them. Allergies? Medications? OB/GYN? Diseases? I don't remember half of what I said, or if I even heard the questions. My head was full of Ted and the prophecy.

Shortly, a doctor came to me in the waiting room. Shannon's doctor was too far away. They needed my permission to administer obstetrical care. Shannon was in critical condition. The baby had no pulse. Deep in my core, I knew Wren was dead, but they hoped to force a heartbeat with an experimental drug. Doctor Baru Faguma, part of the medical team, acknowledged my strength. He thanked me for the opportunity to try and save my grandson. Even though he voiced the sentiment, there was no encouragement in his words.

Chapter 32: *The Other Side*

Ted sat opposite me. Time was endless as I waited. I ignored him as best I could; he was nothing. He had committed to my grandson's death and here we were, waiting for fate to confirm it. I could not challenge him here, and what if I could; so what? I rocked in the seat and looked at the door. Ted spoke.

"You are out of harmony, Grace. You must focus on the matter at hand."

I stared at him as if I'd lost my mind. He continued talking. "It is time for your journey and your decision. You have been granted permission to see what only the dead may witness. Do you accept?"

"What can the dead show me, you maggot?"

"Hope."

I got up and paced to the double doors that hid my child from my arms. My head hurt. I don't know when it happened, or how, but as I looked through the panes, I began moving through a tunnel so black I felt blind. There were no walls, only a trickling sound of water beneath my feet.

The further I go into the tunnel, the less I feel anger towards Ted. I see a tiny speck of light ahead. It doesn't get any larger as I approach, but intensifies to a golden hue as I arrive at the break in darkness. I push on its softness. The force transports me inside.

My eyes adjust to a circular, mirrored wall, hazy like the bathroom after a hot shower. I swipe a streak with my hand. A teenage girl is singing in the field as she breaks tobacco leaves from their stalks, and joins them with others under her arm. Other visions followed.

"What is this place?"

"It is the *Realm of Remembrance*," Ted said. "It is the first stop in our transformation. Every person sees whatever he or she wants to see, or needs to see about their past. The *Realm of Remembrance* is a reflecting pool of moments in your life."

"Who were those people?"

"Let's continue."

Literally, in the blink of an eye I am back in the tunnel but it's lit enough that I can see my hands in front of me; the water still beneath my feet. I come to a ten-foot door surrounded by giant crystal columns. It's like an Egyptian Palace. Metal birds, their wings in flight, adorn each side of the door. Each bird holds a seed in its beak.

The door moves with ease, as if it is a mere thought bending to my will. Inside is a circular room just large enough for a bed. Above me is what looks to be a sky of clover. The spine of each leaf emits a smoky luminance. The walls are the color of the ocean. A thin sheet of water flowing across it feels like velvet.

A bed of white orchids floats in the center of the room. Two small animals serve as pillows. They are furry like bunnies, but big as lions. They appear to be sleeping; I can't see their faces. This delicate room is heavy with sadness.

I recline on the orchid bed. The animals enclose me in fur. I can feel their hearts beating. The sound of water trickles all around the room. I almost fall sleep. My mind empties.

Four colors shape themselves into a circle above me like the rings of Saturn. Sparkling gold. Translucent black, shimmering silver, and pearly white. In hypnotic motion, the colors swirl until they become mist.

In quick succession, the images from the Realm of Remembrance play in fast forward in my mind. I see every detail of what happened beyond the moment.

The strongest vision of all is a child stolen from the womb of its mother. He is abandoned in a hospital where it endures endless experiments. The thief spends his nights telling himself he did the right thing until the liquor blurs all thoughts of the child he took from his sister.

I curled myself within the nest of breathing fur and breaking hearts and cry. I weep until my tears wash across the marble floor, join the pond surrounding me, and become the wall of water flowing down the room. Instantly, I know. "This room is the *Temple of Tears* isn't it," I said to Ted.

"Every soul comes here to repent the hurt they've caused and the hurt caused them," Ted said. "Here, we witness the misfortunes of our lives—the transgressor and the transgressed. The wrongs done and the disadvantage heaped upon innocence. In this room every human being answers to itself," he said. "In this place, we see the roads not taken, name the regrets, and accept the consequences of selfishness. When I came, I saw all the things I did to your grandmother. I felt all the pain I caused every woman

I ever dated. I saw the effects of taking a life from the world. It took me a long time to accept who I had been. Eventually, we leave that person here in the arms of Wisdom and Compassion. By grace, we are purged and made clean again."

"But the images I saw were not my life?"

"It is not your time. These are the lives of those who have or will cross your path. You will help them, or not," Ted said. "Time will tell."

Chapter 33: *Fate*

Doctor Faguma tapped on my shoulder. "Your daughter will be fine," he said. "The bullet missed any vital organs."

I wiped tears from my face. "And her child," I asked, when he didn't offer.

"I'm afraid we were not as fortunate."

My breathing stopped. I saw Dr. Faguma's mouth moving but I didn't hear any other words until I heard him calling my name.

"The bullet entered the child's abdomen. There were no vitals. However, we delivered the fetus but did not separate it from the mother. We removed the bullet and returned the child to the womb."

"But why," I asked. "You just said he died."

"The experimental compound I mentioned has had remarkable results in the past. I happened to be here for another procedure. We injected the child with the compound and will continue treatment over the next twenty-four hours."

"I don't understand," I said.

"If all goes well, the compound will restart the baby's heart."

I held my hand to my mouth. "Oh, my God." Tears welled again at that possibility.

Dr. Faguma continued. "Because this is a highly sensitive procedure, we must keep the mother in a coma until we know how the child responds. I have to get back now. The nurse will take you to your daughter shortly."

Chapter 34: *The Letter*

After the first week, I spent a lot of time in the hospital's garden planted by volunteers. A small plaque announced the organization's name. I prayed there amid small bronze and iron statues of children at play. Here, the world seemed right.

I heard Nola's voice outside Shannon's room when I returned. I stood outside the door and listened, partly because I wanted to hold onto the peace I had attained in the garden, partly because she was reading to Shannon. The words I heard washed over me until they felt like clothes in a rainstorm.

.... We had a good Thanksgiving. We had turkey and cranberry sauce and sweet potato pie. Lyn still looks like a tick. We wish you could be here.

We spent the whole weekend with Grandma Mattie. She came to get us when we got home from school. Lyn and I helped her cook. Grandma Mattie tells us about our father every time we visit. I like her stories. She says we look like him. I asked her who Dillon looks like. She said, 'another side of the family'. I tell her we haven't met anyone who looks like him. They must live far away. Are they in New York where you are?

As you know, Christmas is coming. Will you be coming home? Lyn wants a guitar. Grandma Mattie said our father played the guitar. Dillon says he wants toy guns and a camera. Grandma said we'll do good to have food on the table.

We killed a big hog last month and the garden did really good this year. My fingers are still sore. As for me, all I want is to have you here with us. Maybe Santa can bring the things for Lyn and Dillon. But you can bring my gift. That's all I want. We miss you.

Love,

Grace

PS: If you want to, you can bring me a book that I don't have to take back to the Library. I like Cinderella. It will be my very own. Thanks Momma. I love you.

Silence followed. Shortly, I heard Nola say, 'I came back to her Shannon; you have to come back, too.' My chest felt as tight as a hooker's dress. I had written that letter when I was ten years old.

I looked through the window. Nola's back was to me but I could tell she was staring at the letter. She shuffled the pages until they returned to the position in which they'd rested all these years. She slid the faded envelope back into its batch and placed the lid back on the box. Nola shifted inside the impression she'd made on the corner of the bed. She rubbed her fingers across her palms. The movements could have been Braille except Mama didn't know the language. I then heard her say, 'I took too long'. Nervous laughter made her reach for the box of tissue. She dabbed her eyes, and said, "You get well in there, sweetheart, come back soon. Your mama needs you."

Chapter 35: *Dillon*

.Dillon was the baby Mama left behind. We called him Dell. He cried for his mother every night for months after she left. He cried about everything; seemed like for no other reason than he had lungs. He'd cry till his gray eyes were puffballs for hours after he'd stopped. I thought his crying had washed the brown color right out. Little ringlets at the nape of his neck and around his forehead stuck to him from the wetness. His light skin turned red.

Dell was allergic to everything. He'd break out in hives if the temperature changed, and it did, often. Grandmother's cure was two heaping teaspoons of Milk of Magnesia. Milk of Magnesia, Castor Oil, rubbing alcohol, BC Powder and Vicks Vapor Rub were the only residents in grandmother's medicine chest. If they couldn't cure it, a good sweat with a piece of fatback strapped to the chest was the next resort.

Dillon hated the chalky taste of Milk of Magnesia, rightfully so. It would seep through his lips in his efforts not to swallow. For gagging, he got yanked off the floor by one arm and spanked; his little legs kicked the air.

I consoled him after his bouts with Grandmother. His sniffles were so hard it seemed he'd stopped breathing. One day, while rocking the bed to comfort him, I noticed the blue and white label on the bottle Grandmother had left behind. I was reading everything by now, pure habit, almost instinct. I took the bottle from the dresser and studied it closer. Surprisingly, I discovered a word I had not seen on the bottle before. I got a blue crayon, to match the label, and covered all the letters but three. I lifted Dell to my little lap. I held the bottle in front of him, pointed to each letter and spelled: M...O...M.. " Do you know what that spells," I asked in my loving, eight-year-old, big sister voice.

Dell shook his head as he sucked up waterfall tears.

"Mom," I told him. "It spells mom."

Dell looked up at me and sniffled in shorter notes. Except for the occasional jerk, his chest stopped heaving. He pointed a finger to the bottle and repeated the word I had given him. "Mom," he said and laid his head against my tiny chest. I held my little brother in my arms and rocked the four year old until he fell asleep. He looked at the bottle differently after that day.

Chapter 36: *SuKu- Dementia*

The MaeAlice strained to see the young man coming towards her. Her lips trembled. She reached out her hand as he sat at the foot of her bed. He touched her. A frightened smile gave way to tears. She called his name. "Daniel? Daniel?" And her mind answered, yes, even though it was not the name he spoke to her in reply.

MaeAlice dismissed everyone else from her presence so they could be alone. She pulled him to her fragile arms and summoned all her strength to hold him. "I'm so glad you came," she whispered. "I'm so sorry. But I made it right. I want you to know what I did. I want you to know I made it right."

The secret she'd kept all these years swelled like a container of milk left too long. It needed release. And so it began. She returned to the night the secret got its birth; the one Grace kept for her. The one that ate her soul.

Chapter 37: *SuKu - The Gift*

The Slang and Raymond Solder began the search for Ted the day after Daniel died. As much as The Ray liked Slang, he cared equally less for Daniel. Too arrogant, he thought. But he liked MaeAlice.

Ray was Slang's thieving partner; his specialty was houses and he took his job seriously. Sometimes he took stuff back just to see if he could. He didn't steal in Blessing because many had nothing worth taking—except dignity. That, he couldn't take back. Neither could it be replaced. Ray stole in other towns from white folk.

"White folk got this air that lets them think nothing bad ever happen to 'em," he'd said. "Make people think their spirit can't be broken."

The Ray would pick a house based on the car in the driveway or clothes the family wore. How they treated black folk. He liked taking from arrogant white folks best. Made them squeeze their heads and wring their hands. Made them afraid.

Once in a while he'd have to teach a black family, too. 'Do-ditty', he called them. "Them wanna forget they got kin-folk still sleeping four to a bed. Putting on airs. Turning their heads from black folk just like them."

Yes. Mister and Misses Do-ditty had to come down a peg, too. "They need to remember what it is to work hard and have nothing to show for it."

While he knew practically everyone in Blessing, not many knew Ray; he was an enigma; a shadow almost. Ray didn't talk much about himself or anything else. Even when he did a job with Slang, they'd plan it; do it, but not utter a word about it when the job was done. Those who even bothered to wonder suspected Ray stole for a living, but no one knew for sure. Except Slang. And what Slang knew, Daniel knew.

The Ray knew people. He was older than Slang but took a liking to him. He saw potential and tested what The Slang called 'a proclivity for thievery'. Slang passed easily and Ray began sharing tricks of the trade with his protégé, but left some lessons open-ended.

"Some things you learn on your own," he told Slang. "Whatever job you do, find a way to make it your own. Even if a thousand people do the same job, the way you do it should be personal," he offered. "Make what you do a work of art. People might despise what you do, but if it's art, they'll admire the way you do it. They'll respect the results."

The Ray responded to the confused look on Slang's face. "A person becomes good at what he does for one of three reasons. He's born to do it; he needs to do it; or he wants to do it. No matter which of those is true the result is the same."

"Hey man," Slang jived, "a job is a job. No reason I know 'cept ta get paid. And the reason behind that is to get laid."

"That's my point," Ray agreed. "You *need* money to get something you *want* more."

The Slang still didn't get it. "Man, you gotta break that down 'coz you just put me in the lost and found."

"Who's the best football player you know?"

102

"Jim Brown!" Slang yelled. "That brah'tha can put it down!"

"Jim Brown is good because he was born with talent. But the first thing that happened is somebody put a ball in his hand. Eventually, he needed to play, wanted it so bad, he was bad."

"Oh... I see," Slang chimed. "Like my uncle Joe is good at fixing cars 'coz his daddy told him he needed something the man couldn't control for his living. Then everyday, he put a wrench in his hand and didn't let him do nothing else." He thought on it for a while. "Man, if it runs and breaks down, Unk can put it back on the ground."

"Exactly," The Ray replied.

Proud Slang continued. "Oh... and it's because Vanessa likes sex so much that she's the best ho for miles around. The girl loves her work," he smiled. "And I do admire that."

As the memory of Vanessa's skill faded, he added, "Okay, I see. My man was born to play, Vanessa loves to fuck, and both are damn good. I get it. Like you said, no different." Slang smiled again and propped in his chair. "Hey man, which category are you? Born to? Want to? Need to?"

The Ray didn't answer. He leaned in his chair and opened the refrigerator door. He set two beer bottles on the metal table with the fake marble top and pushed one to Slang. Ray put the glass tube to his mouth, tossed his head back, and poured without his lips touching the rim. The back of his throat closed, forcing his cheeks to fill. Slang followed suit except he sipped. Didn't like the burn from guzzling.

When Slang turned to dispose of his bottle cap, he saw the makeshift shelf over the kitchen sink lined with medicine bottles. His question to Ray became obvious. Mrs. Solder was in and out of hospitals since Ray was twelve years old.

Ray never talked about how he provided for his mother. He never bragged about the houses he robbed. Jail was not an option. Had life been different, he might have been a lawyer, like Perry Mason. Every week, Ray saw justice prevail. He learned wrongs could be made right, even when things looked bad. What happened to his mother was wrong; stealing could help make it right. And now, another mother needed a tilt towards justice. He could not refuse.

Chapter 38: *SuKu - Caught*

 The Slang made good his promise. He found Ted. On Sunday night, two days after Daniel was covered with dirt, they paid a visit.

The Ted lay in bed in the four-room house set back in the woods. A dirt-driven path showed the way. Even so, a visitor had to pay attention. Trails that went nowhere became hiding places for little boys getting little girls in trouble. Dust roads ended in ragged fields where scraggy weeds reclaimed their territory. The two heard canned laughter from a television show.

"Cuz, he's gotta to be watching fuzz on that damn thing this deep in the woods," Slang said.

The owner lived here with her teenaged son. She worked third shift and the son was out getting laid. It was Sunday night, not much else to do. Living this far in the boondocks, the two never expected trouble so took few precautions to protect themselves or their property.

The Ted's back was to the door. "Well, ain't this cozy," said a voice from behind. He jumped, and turned his head to see Ray standing in the doorway. Ted's mouth opened, a small gasp escaped. The silver glow from the TV exaggerated the gloss on the white of his eyes.

"What's that look on your face," Ray said. The metal bed squeaked as The Ted tried to put a name to the voice.

"All that TV and what the hell do you see? Not a damn thang," Ray's eyes scanned Ted. His sun brown skin was covered in bruises. Purple and black splotches exposed themselves from underneath the gall shirt. Slick dress pants hid the rest.

"Who the hell are you," Ted asked, getting his bare feet to the floor. He caught a solid right blow to his face as he moved towards Ray. The blow sent him back to the bed. It squawked louder from the force hitting worn metal springs.

"Don't matter who I am you sack of shit," Ray told him. "But you might be interested in the fella behind me."

Slang stepped in the doorway gripping a baseball bat. Ted's legs got a message from his brain. Run! Before he could find the place he kept his strength, the sound of wood cracking bone echoed off the walls. The bat vibrated. Ted yelled and fell to the floor.

"Don't worry, shit head, we ain't gonna kill yo' sorry ass; though I do believe the Good Book says an eye for an eye. Heard the preacher say that once. You do believe in the Good Book, don't cha?" Slang pulled a piece of rope from his pocket and tied Ted's hands behind his back. Without speaking to anyone in particular, he commented, "I never got the gist of that verse till a week ago."

Ted's feet were next. In too much pain to protest, he lay on the floor in a hump. Slang's disgust made him spit.

It landed near Ted's face, forcing him to look up at his captors.

"I guess you happy, you little faggot," directing his words to Slang. He didn't know Ray, so paid him no mind. You got me. So, what you gonna do, fuck me," he taunted. "Isn't that what that dead little bastard did for you?"

Slang kicked him in the back with the same hatred as Daniel had done. He knelt on one knee in Ted's face to see the pain up close.

"Let's do this, partner," Ray intervened. We ain't got time to play with this shit."

Slang leaned down and whispered to Ted. "Ain't nothing I'd enjoy more than ripping out your heart and dancing to the beat, you son-of-a-bitch."

Instead, Slang pulled a bag containing a loose white powder from his jacket. He didn't do drugs but he had friends. His friends had connections. Ray held Ted's mouth open.

"Swallow, asshole," Slang demanded. Ted had to obey; the powder was halfway down his throat from his sucking in oxygen to send to his aching leg. The scattered powder covered his nose and mouth; remnants flew on the billow from his nostrils.

When he stopped coughing, Ted spoke. "What now, little bastard, you gonna watch me die?"

"Oh no," Slang taunted. "Remember, we ain't gon' kill ya. You got a trip to take. That's to make sure we getcha there, calm like. If you tried anything, I'd be forced to stomp you to the hell you gon' call home sooner than expected."

"You want me to scream, little mud'a-fucka. Don't hold your breath. I heard enough screaming two days ago to hold me." Ted saw the reaction on Slang's face. "Yeah, I went to the send-off." Ted laughed and then coughed. "I wanted to be there for my woman. She needed me, don't you think?"

The slurred words bit Slang like a rabid dog. He stomped Ted's chest, sat on the sagging bed and brutally anchored his foot against Ted's neck. "You could die now, you son-of-a-bitch," he said through clenched teeth. "But you'd miss the surprise."

Ray leaned against the doorframe and watched the powder take effect. They dragged Ted by his elbows and tossed him forward. He fell like a chunk of wood in the back of the truck. The cocaine eased the pain in his chest and legs. Slang drove while Ray sat in the back and kept an eye on the bounty, secure in the fact that Ted would see justice.

Chapter 39: *SuKu - The Dream*

The Ted drifted deeper into darkness with each bump. The pain rolled away with each swerve. The trauma of his situation was replaced with visions of the past. Grace was one of them. That little girl warmed something inside him, made him smile.

MaeAlice was there, in his dream. Alone, in their room, she lay beside him, exploring his chest with her hand. At times like this, she felt as young as he. In their private space, he told her stories. "When Nola comes back, we're packing up and getting out of here." He told her all his plans. "We can travel for months to any place you can dream. There'll be no drinks to sell, no yards to rake, no tobacco fields. Just you and me. People will wait on you.

Someone will make your bed and dinner will come on a plate with a bright silver dome to keep the flies away."

"And just how we gon' do all that?" she asked.

"Well, maybe I've got a suitcase full of money, a whole suitcase full," he whispered back.

The MaeAlice laughed. She loved his stories; found comfort in them because she was in his arms. He talked about his best friend, Lawrence, and the things they had done for fun. He told her stories from the salon. But the one where they traveled to places she'd never seen; where she was taken care of, she loved most.

Ted's vision included scenes from outside their private time, too. He'd tell the children things to do and MaeAlice would stop them. Often, they'd argue about how she treated them, and she'd remind him who she was. Ted wanted to help but didn't know how. Thoughts of her hidden gentleness, the way she touched him, kept him searching. The sadness in Grace's voice made him stay.

Soon, their private talks ended. MaeAlice no longer touched him and he no longer cared. He got her affections elsewhere. He made sure she knew.

And then there was Daniel. He watched him become a man to defend a threat. Shortly, all the visions were gone. Darkness consumed him completely.

Chapter 40: *SuKu - Delivered*

It was 12:53AM when she heard the truck outside. The house was still. No customers came tonight out of respect. This was the unspoken ritual surrounding death. The family is given a period of stillness, of reverent solitude. The living would return to their routine tomorrow, but not tonight.

The Grace was a light sleeper and the rattling sound of the truck opened her eyes. The truck's engine stopped grumbling. Grace listened for the doorbell but it didn't ring. Instead, she heard careful raps on the windowpane at the back door. The visitor was not a customer.

The MaeAlice was not expecting anyone either. She heard the smothered clacking sounds but showed no interest in its rapper. Having finally been able to close her eyes, she hoped the intruder would leave. But the tapping had moved to her bedroom window. A voice got her attention.

MaeAlice turned the handle that opened the rollout slats. A burst of cool air broke the spell of surrender. She grabbed at the neck of her nightgown with one hand and reached for her thick cotton robe with the other.

"Miss Mae. Go to the backdoor. Hurry." She heard Slang's feet hit the dirt as he leapt off the porch. MaeAlice found the slippers she'd made out of discarded shoes. She dragged across the linoleum floor towards the back door where The Slang waited. She pulled back the fabric, knowing it was Slang but wanting to see his face anyway. On the step below him, she saw Ray. MaeAlice opened the door.

"What in heaven's name you two doing here this time of night?" She didn't ask them in.

"I know Mama Mae," Slang answered, "but this is exactly the night for what I brought you. It's on the truck. Come look."

"If you stole something, now is not the time! I just buried my child."

Slang took MaeAlice's hand and pulled her gently down the steps. She didn't resist. In her mind, she'd begun to figure what she'd do with the chicken and pork chops they'd stolen. Her freezer was already brimmed with payments he'd made for one reason or another. When they reached the truck, Slang said nothing; neither did she. A chill went through her body and settled in her eyes.

Chapter 41: *SuKu - Awake*

Ted awoke to the drug wearing off. His head felt like a nail jammed through the eye of a needle. His leg throbbed; his head ached. Half conscious, he looked around, trying to find something he recognized. The smell of fresh cut oak and pine filled his nostrils from every direction. It was dark inside and out. Small slits of moonlight peeked through rejected lumber. The moon was full; he could see that. He heard noises. Grunts. Animal sounds. The rich stench registered hogs. He tried moving but couldn't. His hands were still tied behind his back. The rope that bound his feet was stretched to a post in one corner of the stall. A rope around his neck was secured to another. Duct tape gagged his mouth. The same material bound him at the knees. Before passing out in the truck, he had heard Slang talking. The words sounded far in the distance. Only one word penetrated his fading consciousness: MaeAlice.

As it fully registered, she was there, standing over him, her body in fragments through the slits of lumber. She pushed aside the boards and looked down on him. He tried speaking but the words stuck in his mouth and came through his nose in bursts of gobbled air. He tried kicking and thrashing from side to side but that only brought more pain. MaeAlice left. Ted heard the back door close. Shortly, she was back.

He heard the sound of metal pressing into dirt. Digging. There were other sounds outside his prison but the digging was the only one that mattered. One shovel. He leaned his head to peek out. She'd put on a pair of men's work pants and long sleeved shirt. He assumed the shirt was flannel. She had several of them in different colors and variations of plaid. She wore no jacket even though it was cooler than usual tonight for October in North Carolina. Indian Summer had peaked. Winter was approaching.

The Ted saw MaeAlice lift her foot and press hard against the curled wedge of steel. The shovel's blade pierced the dirt with little resistance. He was taken aback that he'd never noticed how natural she looked with some tool in her hand. The shovel was an extension of her, was committed to her, like the day he first saw her uprooting weeds with a hoe. The rope tugged on his neck but he could see the truck was gone. He was alone with his jilted lover. The mother of the boy he killed a week ago. And she was digging.

The digging stopped. The shovel fell onto the woodpile nearby. She'd only dug about fifteen minutes; it couldn't be his grave. A heavy gust of wind left his lungs through his nostrils and came out as relief. MaeAlice picked up an armful of wood and went inside.

She was back. She pushed the slab over him into the mud. Ted saw the knife in her hand and froze. MaeAlice cut the rope holding his legs. Both ends of the stall had latching doors. One faced the pigpen to coax the animal in and the other faced the yard to drag him out. She undid the outside latch. His terror subsided. His legs were still bound together but he could bend his knees. He quickly found he'd traded one agony for a bigger one. Pain seared through him like lightening striking the ground. MaeAlice put one foot inside the stall. Pressing a knee into his chest to steady herself, she cut the rope strangling his neck. The pain vibrated off his ribcage in search of a way out. He knew she wasn't threatening him with the gesture; she didn't regard him at all. Besides, she had a knife and Ted was no fool. If it were in her mind, she'd use it.

The MaeAlice dragged Ted by the rope binding his feet. She held the knife securely in the other fist, just in case. His body thumped across the floorboards and plopped to the ground. The drug was leaving his system quicker than startled roaches. He pressed his eyes shut hard, trying to slow the pain. His broken leg throbbed like a racing heartbeat. Tears washed down the sides of his face and collected behind his ears. He looked up to see the seven-foot workhorse over him. Panic struck again. He felt it, mildly at first, when he heard her digging. Maybe I'm hallucinating, he thought. Must be the drugs. A bad trip. That's what this is. Yes, a bad trip, he said, comforting himself until he heard the digging again. Fear gripped his chest, awakening every nerve in his body. Maybe she's digging potatoes. No, she's not digging. She's not.

Eventually, Ted heard the shovel fall onto the woodpile again; the metal banged against dry logs. The MaeAlice passed another rope between his legs and tied it in a knot. Ted thrashed around on the ground. He tried to yell but choked on his words. No one would hear him; the nearest neighbor was a quarter mile away. The choking burned in his chest. Snot rushed from his nose. His eyes watered more.

The MaeAlice slung the rope across the top beam. She went to the other side and pulled, hoisting Ted's six-foot frame in the air. She pulled until he was completely off the ground, then, wrapped the length of the rope around a side beam, knotting it off. It was then that Ted saw the hole she'd dug directly beneath his head.

The moon shone on Ted's face. He was covered with dirt, snot and tears. It was one-forty in the morning by MaeAlice's calculations. About the same time Slang had banged on her door a week ago and said her son had been shot. It was just three nights ago that Olivia told her who did it. Less than two days ago, she buried her son. The thing that got loose in her head the night of his death came back, fully grown.

The MaeAlice rolled a log from the woodpile and took a seat on it directly in front of Ted. He wiggled and huffed but it didn't matter. MaeAlice saw something in his eyes, an intensity that mesmerized her until she named it: fear. She'd never seen it in him before. Something like it she'd witnessed in the face of others from time to time, but this brand of fear was new to her.

"You wanna tell me what happened, I guess," she said. "But your version don't matter." She spoke as if talking to herself. Her voice was low, sad, like a misery so old it had no beginning. "You took from me. You started taking from me the day I laid eyes on you. You took my money and my friends. You took my food, my love. You took my pride. All I ever did was give. I gave it all willing; and you took. You never gave nothing back. But now, you took my child, my only son. I didn't give you that. He was the one thing I gave my husband that he truly wanted. But even he wasn't enough; that wasn't the end of your taking. Now, because of you, I won't see my daughter again neither." The Mae-Alice leaned into him. "You think you can take and never have to pay? Well, It's my turn to take."

Ted gurgled and wiggled. The seven-foot beams squeaked under his weight. MaeAlice rose from her seat on the log. She walked behind him and knelt on the ground, resting her head in the small of his back. MaeAlice wrapped one arm around his waist and ran her hand from his crotch to his neck. His body felt good. She remembered how he felt on top of her, his strong young body moving, pushing. She thought of him resting his head on her sagging breast. She remembered. MaeAlice caressed him one last time, holding him firmly as he squirmed. She extended his neck downward, stretching it tightly. She raised her other arm up. Ted saw a glitter of silver in the midnight light. The knife. Coming towards him like a pendulum. His eyes locked shut. The last thing he saw was the blade; the last thing he felt was vengeance. It flowed from his neck across his face into the earthen goblet below. The liquid washed through his mangled processed hair in dark gushes until it slowed to a trickle and stopped.

Tears heavy as the blood that covered Ted's face filled MaeAlice's eyes. She sat on the ground behind him until she could feel her legs. She cut the tape binding his hands and knees. His arms fell like a broken pump handle, striking the ground and staying there. She pulled his muddy undershirt down his arms. With the sharp of the knife, she stabbed him in the soft of his belly and forced the knife down.

Heat gushed from the gash and sprayed her face with its warmth. She stuck the knife in the side of the beam and with both hands, pulled the organs from his body. She flung the contents into the pigpen. The animals grunted and moved towards the sloshing sound. Afterwards, she filled in the hole she'd dug with the dirt she'd taken from it; sealing it tightly so nothing disturbed his sacrifice.

MaeAlice loosed the rope and let Ted drop. She pulled at his pants but the swollen leg filled the cavity. She made a slit at the cuff with the knife and ripped the fabric with her bare hands. As usual, no underwear. She liked that about him; that he dared. She couldn't help but touch his skin and remember.

She threw the pants in the same direction as the shirt and dragged the dead weight to the stump that was once a hickory tree. She picked up the ax and let it fall. Over and over.

Chapter 42: *Suku- The Fire*

Grace felt the heat coming from her Grandmother's room. She even smelled it. It made a roaring, sucking sound. It lapped and crackled and hissed. She'd heard the fire sing before but this was different.

MaeAlice made several trips to the woodpile. The echo of the ax was not the sound the blade usually made when it cut through wood. Several thumps came in succession, then silence. Next came the iron gate of the furnace opening. The flame roared. The gate closed.

Grace got up and walked down the hallway. MaeAlice's body emerged from her room, bent and haggard. She was covered in the dark film Grace had seen on Olivia's dress a week ago. "Granny, are you all right?" she asked.

MaeAlice turned slowly; she didn't expect to see Grace there but had no other reaction either way. She shook her head, no. And in the same rare voice MaeAlice used the night that Daniel died, she said, "Go back to bed, baby." The MaeAlice walked back to the kitchen, down the six cinder block steps and back to the woodpile. More thumping followed, and then, the iron gate. As the fire sucked oxygen from the room, a shrill pierced the air.

It was three-twenty in the morning before The MaeAlice was done. She stripped and stuffed the clothes into the mouth of the furnace. She went naked to the bathroom. The water washed over her. When she was clean, she wrapped herself in a blanket and cried.

Tomorrow, she would scatter his ashes in her garden. The beans would feed on his remains just as the pigs had fed on his liver. Tonight, she fed on the flames.

Chapter 43 : *Suku - Done*

MaeAlice looked into her Daniel's eyes. Tears slid down her cheeks and settled into the lines and grooves of time and grief. "Do you think God will forgive me?"

Malice took the frail woman into his arms and rocked her amid tears of his own, and kisses of absolution.

Chapter 44: *Wren's Arrival*

Shannon slept. And slept. I prayed.

Eight days from the shooting, Dr. Fugama gave me the news. The baby was responding exceedingly well. In fact, he said the bullet wound was nearly healed. Even in her coma, Shannon was working. This was her gift—she'd healed herself many times as a child. Going into medicine was a natural fit.

Nine days later, Shannon awoke. The hospital kept her a few more days to ensure she and the baby had no adverse effects. They were labeled miracles.

Two weeks later, to our surprise, Shannon delivered a beautiful baby girl. A girl? All testing prior to the shooting said Wren was a boy. But here we were, with the first-born female of the first-born female of generations of first-born women before her. I had seen Wren in my vision, as a beautiful young woman, the Voice declared it so, still, I was as stunned as Shannon.

Dr. Fugama explained it as a fluke in the previous tests, but I knew he was lying. I read him. If was difficult, but my sense was it had something to do with the injections. I pulled him aside and asked.

"Gender assignment is not possible, yet." He assured me the compound was not for that purpose. "Your daughter presented a unique opportunity to test the material further. It is amazing that the child responded," he said. "We've not had good results on unborn children in the past."

His last sentence repeated in my head. What had he done with unborn children? Right now, the past was of no concern to me. "We are grateful you were here, Doctor Fugama." I could not tell him of Shannon's role in his miracle, or the vision I had that told me she and the baby would survive.

I returned to the room to find Ted at Shannon's bed. "Shannon can't see me; I did not want to upset her," he said. "Wren is beautiful."

"How dare you," I thought back.

"Grace, it is time to finish why I am here."

"You wanted Wren dead."

"No, I told you the boy Wren had to die. That was so this little gift could be born."

"So the legacy continues."

"As it must. This little girl has a significant task ahead, Grace, a challenge that will redefine what it means to be human. But more on that later. Right now, we have to go. Your grandmother is almost done."

Chapter 45: *Truth is Ugly*

Sunday opened its arms with the gift of sunshine that dried the morning dew. Shannon slept as Nola and Jim prepared for church. I watched the birds play from the kitchen window while I poured a glass of juice. The phone rang. "I got it," I called, to no one in particular. "Buenos Dais!"

"And just when did you learn Spanish?"

" Gotta keep up, Aunt Liv. The French I learned way back is useless. How are you this beautiful morning? What's up?"

"I'm in a good mood. Come have breakfast with me. Well, it'll be brunch actually, and you can tell me all about some dream you must have had. What'da'ya' say? Champagne brunch?"

Although cheerful, the message in her voice told me two things; Aunt Olivia needed company, and, she wanted to talk. Since she didn't invite Shannon, I was to come alone. "You think God will mind if we have champagne on Sunday?"

"It is the drink of the gods, ain't it?"

"No, Aunt Liv; that's wine."

"Wine, champagne, same grape."

I laughed, "See you in a few."

The TV was on in Nola's room. A gospel song wafted through the cracked door, heavy on the bass and high on soprano. Not a sound I enjoyed but most of the black churchgoing population would be patting their feet to similar sounds all across the south in about an hour. I looked in on Shannon. Little Wren kept her up last night so she was down for a while longer. I found Grandma staring at the popcorn ceiling.

"Look at what I got Granny."

Grandmother stretched her lips enough to suggest a smile. I guided the straw to her mouth. The juice moved slowly upward, slid back, and climbed again. It reached Grandmother's throat. She winced; the first passage was always the hardest.

"Good?" Another wince and a smile showed her agreement. I reorganized the covers and kissed her cheek. Grandmother whispered to me, "Thank you." At first I thought she meant for the juice, but the look in her eyes told me differently. I whispered back, "You're welcome, Granny."

~ o ~

Olivia had placed a platter of melons and blueberries on the table. Two glasses of cranberry mimosa fizzed. I remembered the last time I made this trip. Shannon and I learned her son would die. We raced away from here trying to outrun the truth, only to meet it in the place we were racing to. Baby boy Wren died and was returned to us as Wren, baby girl, deliverer of some fate to come. When the front door swung open and Olivia emerged in an African robe, I tucked the thoughts away.

119

"You look beautiful." I scanned my sweatshirt and shorts. "Please forgive this peasant in your presence."

"Sit down, girl. I was thinking of giving it to you anyway; just wanted your reaction. It's yours."

"Where on earth will I wear something that spectacular?"

"To bed, for all I care," Olivia said. "Speaking of which, how did you sleep last night?"

Olivia munched a bagel and waited. I processed what should have been my response but selected a different reply. "Wren was fussy. Granny had a rough night. She's declined a lot, lately."

"Yeah, she made a serious nose-dive when Shannon was shot. We never told her, but it was like she knew, like there was a change in the Universe that binds y'all."

"Aunt Liv, I never thanked you for coming to Virginia and sitting with me."

"Girl, now where else would I have been? Somebody had to watch over your soul while you watched over that beautiful baby. That's partly why I asked you to come. I want to apologize for taking off like that. You were right. We don't always get a chance to resolve things. It was time to make peace with Momma. I haven't said the words, but I've tried to be a better daughter. I haven't fully let go, but I'm working on it. Now, you need to do the same."

"Peace with what?"

"Don't go getting snippy with me. Your mother, that's what." Olivia answered back, with equal combat. She speared a piece of cantaloupe and held it midair. "You've asked me many times why your mother left you. I never said. Didn't think it was my place, and you were so young. When Nola came back and you were older, did you ever ask her?"

120

"No, what difference did it make then? As you pointed out, I was older. She came back with a husband and life took a different turn for all of us. Why she left no longer mattered."

Olivia let the melon slide off the knife onto her plate. She gave me her full attention.

"Her letters said she left for work. Apparently she liked it so much she forgot to come back for us." Embarrassed by my anger, I lowered my head. "I'm sorry. I don't know where that came from."

"From feeling abandoned."

I filled my cheeks with melon. Olivia picked up her glass and sipped. "Do you know you use food much like Nola? She uses it to try and put something in, and you to keep something from getting out. It's all about approval for her and denial for you."

How could she say such a thing to me? But I had to consider her observation. Olivia waited but I said nothing.

"During the summer, we helped in the tobacco field. Me, Nola, and Daniel. Mostly me cause Nola was just no good with worms." Those things stung like a lit cigarette. Olivia shuddered at the thought. "Anyway, Nola met your father in that field. He lived in Wink but we attended the same high school. There was only one school for blacks back then. The elementary and high schools were the same building.

"Deacon was two years older than your mother. We'd seen him at school but it wasn't until we were cropping tobacco that summer that Deacon really noticed her. He heard her singing, something to make the work go faster. She was seventeen but had a grown singing voice. Momma wouldn't let us date until we were seventeen; no boys could even come to the house. Some came anyway and ordered beers just to look at us.

"Deacon and your momma got to know each other in that tobacco field. He was Nola's first boyfriend. Everyone thought they were a good couple. Deacon Dupree could play the guitar as if it had shared his mother's womb. Nola had a voice that made you close your eyes just to hold onto the sound. But it was more than that. They really had something together."

Olivia had my attention. I was hearing about my father and mother for the first time, and for the second time that my mother use to sing. Why had I never heard it; why didn't she sing now? I set my questions aside and listened. Somewhere in this story would be why my mother left me. As much as I denied it, I wanted to know. Olivia's next sentence hooked me completely.

"When your father left Nola with the two of you..."

I broke her sentence. "You mean the three of us."

Just listen Grace; it'll make sense when I'm done," Olivia promised. "Deacon's brother was down for a visit. He'd bought a friend with him. They heard Deacon play. All those Dupree boys could play some instrument or another. The friend told Deacon to come to New York with him and he'd have more money than God had saints. Deacon asked your mother to go with him. Nola wouldn't. MaeAlice told Nola that New York was no place to raise children, and everything else she could think of to keep Nola here. It worked." Olivia stared at the expression on my face; saw my body tighten. "What are you thinking, what is it?" Olivia asked.

More pieces; Nola's puzzled conversation at the hospital began to take shape. Still it made no sense. "What happened? I know my father left; what happened?"

Olivia relaxed her concern. "Deacon went to New York. He was beginning to make a name for himself. People absolutely loved him. The man with his brother was a promoter and had gotten Deacon booked into the right circles. Your dad met and played with people who are famous now. A year later, Deacon's mom got a letter from the Armed Services telling him to report for duty. After training, he got thirty days home before shipping out. He helped you celebrate your third birthday. Nine months later, Lyn was born. Deacon didn't make it back; never got to see his daughter."

I felt my heart grow inside my chest. My breathing stopped; my tongue became thick. Dillon was not his son.

Olivia poured champagne into my glass and told me to drink. She gave me time to adjust and for the alcohol to settle in.

"Your mother was a wreck when she got the news that your father's battalion had been captured. Didn't eat for days. About a month later, she went to the trees near the cotton field and sat there. That's where they'd spent a lot of time together, getting to know each other. Nola had taken his guitar and held it in her arms; something, anything to be close to him, you know. She rocked that guitar and began to sing. It was one of those sad, blues songs. Something that made you cry even if you didn't know the words. A car came by. She heard someone behind her and she stopped. Nola knew the local cops because they'd all been to Momma's house at one time or another, but she didn't know this one."

The knot in my chest grew tighter. I forced the glass to my mouth; my hand trembled.

"He was nice enough at first. Wanted to know what was wrong, told her she had a beautiful voice, you know, how pretty she was; both of which was true. Nola didn't answer him. We all had a healthy disdain for cops. Well, Nola ignoring his questions, made him angry. She got up to leave. He grabbed her. Pushed her down. She managed to throw Deacon's guitar to safety."

"'Don't walk away from me, girl'," he said. "'You think I don't know who you are? Damn it, here I am trying to be nice and this is the thanks I get'.

"Nola tried to run. He grabbed her by the arm and threatened to arrest her for trespassing. She had never been to jail, and with two children was not a time to go. She also knew what they were capable of and didn't want to provoke him. It was too late. He pushed her to the ground again. She hit hard. Her dress flew up. She lay there for a second before she could think. By the time she got her senses, she saw his handcuffs in one hand and him loosening his belt with the other. His nightstick and gun dropped to the ground. He dragged her to a small tree and handcuffed her around the base of it."

I heaved; the tightness in my chest wanted out. I ran to the back of the woodpile. Breakfast - the melon, the orange juice; the bagel - poured out. Tears filled my eyes, my nose burned; my stomach rammed itself into my back without mercy.

Olivia ran to the kitchen. I steadied myself on the tree stump, the one that had served a large part of its life as a chopping block. The deep grooves looked like a map to nowhere. The circles of time long gone were still there. It had been here that the old man told me about the rings in a tree.

"Each ring is a period in a tree's life. Some, like this one," he had said, pointing, "Means the tree had a very rough time at this stage in its years. Maybe the weather

124

was bad; maybe cold came and stayed too long. But the tree survived it. Do you understand, little one?"

"Everything becomes a part of who we are," I said.

My answer excited him. "Yes, but there is more. Everything that happened to this tree happened to the others around it, even to the fruit it bore then and the fruit it will bear in the future. Do you understand?" he asked. "You see the bark on that tree over there? It is thick—as thick as this one. You see? That is because that tree was trying to protect itself from whatever happened to this one."

Olivia handed me a warm towel. I covered my mouth to prevent anything else from escaping, or to catch whatever did.

Eventually, Olivia continued. "I made Nola tell me after finding her out there when she hadn't come home. Grace, it was a vile thing he did. But there was nothing we could do about it. Momma may as well been on the post office wall with America's Most Wanted as bad as the police wanted her behind bars. He knew who Nola was. Momma couldn't go to the police and say one of them raped her daughter; he knew that, too. Nola was so ashamed; she left your grandma Mattie's house and moved in with me. That's how Dillon came into this world."

Olivia let me take it all in, process it, digest it; let me replace the food I'd just given up with this information, before she spoke again.

"Grace, deep down, you knew Dillon was different. Maybe not when you were a child, but as you grew up, you saw.

"Nola never fully got over it. Even after Dillon was born, she struggled. The cop must have bragged about it with his friends 'cause they took to riding by at least twice

125

a month and teasing her while she was pregnant. They kept it up even after Dillon was born but not as much.

When Aunt Sahra called, we thought it was a blessing, a way to make it stop and for her to take you all away from here. The only problem was she had to leave you with Momma for a while. I told her she shouldn't but she said it wouldn't be for long. Just till she got settled and found an apartment. She wanted to make sure her job was stable. Problem is, I think she got there and decided something else altogether."

Aunt Liv saw my discomfort and handed me some watermelon to settle my stomach. I chewed the fibers, felt the juices touch the bottom of a deep empty place and echo.

"Grace, I can't excuse what Nola did once she got to New York, but I thought you should know why she left. She'll never tell you this story. I had to drag it out of her. Whether you want to forgive her or not is up to you. But if you're going to make peace with the past, and I think you should, you need to know the circumstances that caused you to feel the way you do about your mother."

Olivia studied the solemn expression on my face. Felt for me. She turned her eyes to the house where we had lived for all those years that Nola was gone. Olivia spoke as if casting a spell. "That place is like a portal to hell and MaeAlice its gatekeeper. There's a lot of bad things soaked in those wall."

Chapter 46: *SuKu - Forgiveness*

The Nola sat with her husband on the long, rolled-back pew. She cradled her Bible between both palms. The minister had announced his sermon and given the congregation a teaser before asking the choir to sing.

"Let's talk about letting go," he said. "Today, I want you to 'Toss Your Sins Upon the Water.'" The reverend held his words for effect. After several obligatory amens from the congregation, he continued. "While the choir sings, I want you to think back. Some of you will think back to yesterday. Some, to last week. And some of you may want to go back years... I want you to find just one; that's all, just one sin, that you want to toss upon the cleansing waters. Something that you'd change if you could. Something, that if God turned back time, it never happened."

The Nola's body tensed. Her fingers gripped the black leather-bound Book. Muffled vocals blended into chords being banged on the church's organ. She didn't hear the title of the song; she didn't hear the words, just sounds strewn around the notes of a tune like bees with different vibrations.

The choir stretched the last syllable of the song and waited for the organ to quiet its last note. Just moments ago, the wine colored robes swayed in unison. The gold stoves that draped down the uniforms moved like wings with each sway. But as the songsters found their seats, they looked like blind boxers punching air. Why doesn't he teach them how to sit down, Nola wondered. The thought was just a diversion. Her mind had already found her moment, and she didn't want to face it.

The preacher rose again and stood behind the podium. He leaned forward, surveying the congregation, letting his eyes rest upon different members long enough to make them fidget. "What if you could change just one sin? One misstep. What if you could go back and do something you should have done? Say something you should have said. How different might your life be today?" He let his words sink into the audience; he straightened his stance and loosened his grip of the podium.

"I was watching television the other night and saw an interesting movie. It was about second chances, making wrong things right. The star of the show had a car accident and was unconscious. While unconscious, he had a dream. In his dream was a woman with whom he had a conversation. The woman said she was taking an accounting of his life. She looked at the pad in her lap and shook her head. 'You've made a lot of mistakes,' she said. You see, sometimes he knew he was missing the mark but did it anyway. Bad decisions people, bad decisions."

"Amen, Reverend, bad decisions," someone chanted.

"The woman went on to tell him there were things he should have done but didn't. Words he should have said that would have made a difference in someone's life, but he withheld those words. Sometimes as punishment, sometimes because he felt it wasn't his place.

"Now, the woman says to him: 'I can strike any sin from your record; it'll be as if it never happened'. Then she looks up from her pad and asks him, 'which will it be?'"

"My people, there's more to sin than doing something wrong. Sometimes, it's also *not* doing something you should have done; not saying something you should have said. Consider this: someone in this room has not reached

128

their full potential because somebody withheld something from them. Can I get an amen?"

The congregation complied in unison with their nodding heads and waving hands held high.

"The woman gave the man one hour to decide. Now this means that the man had to go over everything he'd ever done, and find one thing he didn't want on his account with God. Or, he could put into motion something he should have done but didn't. Something he was supposed to say but pride got in the way. Now, this was a daunting challenge and a wonderful opportunity. I'm not going to tell you how the story ended. It doesn't matter."

That was the last sentence Nola heard from the preacher. She had already taken inventory and found a misstep she wished could be erased, an action she would have given anything to have a different ending.

Her attention returned in time to hear the preacher say, "What that woman offered was forgiveness. Forgiveness people. You'll want to talk to God about it. But don't go to God asking Him to do it. God is not a servant to clean up your mess.

"Then what is it about, Reverend, you ask? What is this forgiveness? Modern language tells us that to forgive means to pardon someone else for something you think they did to you. To grant clemency so you feel better.

"Well, I want to give you another definition. To forgive means: 'on God's behalf I bestow, supply, yield, impart; I pledge to do or say that which serves you.' Not me, but you. It's letting the wrong pass from your heart, whether you did it or it was done to you. We are all servants to each other. We are to 'give' to each other 'for God. For God, we give."

"If saying you're sorry can do good, say it. If accepting an apology moves you from anger to love, accept it. To do so is for "our" good, and our 'good' is God's Will for us.

"What we do with our lives, the deeds we perform, the injury we cause crosses time, crosses the river Jordan. Today, you can stop that ripple you set in motion however long ago. Forgiveness can stop it. It will drop to the river's bed and become a stepping stone."

The preacher's words: 'say you're sorry... stop the ripple', echoed in Nola's head. She thought to herself, if only it could.

Chapter 47: *Buried Treasure*

I got up and walked away. Olivia watched me go quietly to the place I always went as a child. Trees and bush had grown up around the ragged garden of sleep. Headstones leaned in every direction: some to the left, some to the right; others forward, others, back. Time had worn them into submission. Those large enough and planted deep enough held firm, proudly announcing the name of the treasure they were erected to honor.

I found the white willow tree that heard my secrets, listened to me read and absorbed my tears so many years ago. I placed my hand on its bark and traced the grooves with my fingers. Massive roots had surfaced and lay gnarled atop the ground to make a bench. Like it knew I would be back someday, to sit, to talk, to cry. This beautiful thing would be ready to receive me.

I nestled myself against the giant friend and lay my head in its lap. Shame flowed across the bridge of my nose, down the side of my face and formed a caravan of tear-drops down my arm. I wept for my mother, for Olivia, for Grandmother, myself. I understood why Olivia hated her mother. Today brought a glimpse of why Nola resented her, too. As a therapist, I understood that Mama participated in most of those decisions, contributed to her life's direction. But as a daughter and a woman, I felt my mother's pain for something she did not choose.

Amid the tears, I felt someone's presence beside me. It was Ted.

"I'm sorry, Grace," is all he said. And he was. I did not reply, nor did he offer any further consolation. Our silence seemed forever and I wondered why he had come. What else did he need from me? When he finally spoke, it was not a request but a question. A question I was on the verge of asking of myself, but had forgotten when he appeared.

"Freeing Nola from your punishment - what would that mean for you? How would you define her were it not for leaving you? Who would you be if she hadn't?"

I opened my mouth, not sure whether to rally a defense or an attack. Ted ignored my ambivalence.

"Whatever wrong you think she did to you is already forgiven, Grace. Just as your sin towards her."

I felt another surge of anger. In my mind, I heard Olivia telling me to make things right. And here was this 'thing' telling me the same. Even now, I didn't know if I could.

"Grace, the answer is not for me. But it is something you will have to decide. It will take time to make sense of it all, and what it means for you. Meanwhile, I'm here to finish 'her' story."

I looked towards the tombstone that told visitors they stood before Shelia Paxon's resting place. Her small sentry

131

leaned in surrender like the others. But according to Ted, she died in Baltimore and was, no doubt, buried there if her body had been found. I felt my lungs grab for air and didn't realize until that moment that I had been holding my breath.

"Shelia Paxon's body is not there. But the payment for her death is."

I looked at him. "The money?"

"Three hundred thousand dollars in a sealed container buried in that grave. I trust you will use it wisely."

"Oh my god. Blood money!"

"That's one way of seeing it, I suppose" Ted offered. "Perhaps you can also see it as intervention, divine reparation put in motion many years ago for this moment. A ripple on the water, intercepted if you accept it, or going on in time if you don't. You have a service to render, or not. The choice is yours."

Ted stopped and began again in a different tone. "I must go now; I have to meet someone. I trust you and Shannon to make the right decisions."

"Is that what it takes to get you through the pearly gate? To get rid of the money?" The tone was accusatory. Demanding.

"Grace," is all he said.

It wasn't my name, but the obvious disappointment again that made me lower my face from his image. I heard my own righteous indignation and was instantly ashamed. When I looked up, Ted was gone.

For a long time, I stared at the simple granite bearing Shelia Paxon's name. There was over a quarter-million dollars beneath that leaning tombstone.

Like a tape recorder rewound, Ted's last words replayed. My gut wrenched. I ran to the house. Without going in, I yelled to Olivia. "We have to get to Granny. Something's wrong!"

Chapter 48: *Suku - The Call*

At the very instant, The Nola's eyes opened while a deacon said the meditative prayer. A strong sensation surged through her and intensified until it became panic. She grabbed Jim's arm and pulled him towards the aisle. "We have to go," she said, desperately. "Something's wrong. Something's wrong."

The MaeAlice's eyes opened wide. She stared at the ceiling and saw the mystery that was her life. At some point in the story, she screamed.

Chapter 49: *SuKu – The Home Going*

People lined the walkway of Dew Well Baptist Church. Those inside leaned their heads towards the door for a view of the family. The ushers who visited MaeAlice stood in their places to welcome one of their own to this ritual. Some dabbed their dry eyes while resting the other hand upon a behind that was a testament to the vastness of time.

Others held giant arrangements in every color and of almost every flower. Potted lilies lined the walkway. Ivy draped and curled over banisters. Candles flickered around the pulpit. The white double blooms of bloodroots were strewn at the Alter where the casket would soon rest.

Each family member held a cluster of purple daisies. The church bells rang.

The Slang returned to pay his respects. He appeared to have done well. He'd brought land with money from the jewelry he'd stolen and the drugs he'd sold. He'd worked in construction and later started his own business remodeling rooms, restoring floors and rebuilding cabinets. "He didn't seem the type," everyone said. He'd given up stealing and moved away from Blessing after Ray's mother died. Slang, the boy, had seen too many things. He'd witnessed murder, lost a friend, took part in vengeance and stole because he could. From that boy, evolved a man of substance. He'd begun using his given name, Thomas, to leave the past behind.

But today, Slang, the boy, let himself remember the woman he called ma; who took him into her home when he had no place to go. That she treated him as badly as all the other wayward kids she'd helped didn't matter. She hid him from the police. Fed him. And by example, taught him.

When The Reverend Kelly offered the podium for comments, Slang was the first to stand. His eyes rested on the engraving in the banister around the pulpit before he ascended the three steps. *This Do, In Remembrance of Me,* it read.

Once in place, he began. "Anyone who knew Ms. Mae will relate to this story. One Sunday morning when the sun had just begun to peak above the horizon, I don't remember why, but I got up from the chair where I had slept in Daniel's room. Could have been the fog-like heat that woke me. Could have been the beer from the night before that made me go outside. At the bottom of the steps, I stretched to get the knots out of my back. I heard a familiar scratching in the dirt. Nothing stirred this early; even the chickens were still asleep.

"I went to the corner of the house where the sound was coming from. The children raked the yard every day. They even lined up the grooves. They did a good job; Ms. Mae wouldn't take nothing less. But there she was, raking, by the light of a day not even born.

"Naturally, I asked what she was doing."

"What it look like I'm doing?" She snapped back. "Ya'll know how she talked."

'Well, it looks like you raking the yard; but why? Today's Sunday, Mama Mae.' That's what I said. 'Ain't you going to church?' She kept her pace, didn't stop, raked between each word."

'Everything's gotta be clean before I go sit with God. I know it was done yesterday, but I do it myself on Sunday. It's me gotta answer for it. I do it myself; that way I know it's clean. It's gotta be my clean', she insisted and kept on raking.

"As long as I've known her, she'd put her customers out at midnight. I knew she cleaned up after and mopped the house before she went to bed because I'd seen her do it. Even helped her by sweeping sometimes. Now I discovered that every Sunday morning, before the sun even rose, she raked the yard. Trying to make things right before she met with God."

The Slang returned to his seat. No one else saw fit to add to Slang's recollection. What more was there to say?

The Reverend Kelly stood to deliver the eulogy. "This woman was a child of God. She didn't always do what was pleasing in God's sight, but she did what she thought was right. We can't judge her. She was just human, doing the best she could, just like you and me. The only rule book we got is the Bible. And by the time many of us find the Word of God, understand the Word, we've made a terrible mess."

The church echoed Reverend Kelly. "Yes, preacher, a terrible mess."

"But Brothers and Sisters, the 'message' is in the mess. In fact, look at the first-half of the word message, and you'll find 'mess'. And in that mess is the answer. So, take a look at your mess; see what needs to change, what needs to be cleaned. It's never too late to get right with God."

The congregation agreed. "Never too late, never too late."

"Sister Alice worked hard; she worked long. This church never had a more dedicated Sister. But a few days ago, Our Savior sent down His Angel. That Angel leaned over Sister Alice and whispered in her ear. I can almost hear what she said. She said, 'Sister Alice, your work here is done. Your Lord has sent for you. Are you ready to go Home?' Church, sister Alice answered." Reverend Kelly stomped one foot, raised it from the floor and leaned back to let out, "Glory!"

Shannon looked at her mother. She'd told Grace about the scream she'd heard that Sunday morning. The Grace put Shannon's hand in her own and gave it a gentle squeeze. Neither was sure what had happened the moment The MaeAlice died, but certain if an angel spoke, those were not its words.

A sound from the pulpit made them look up. A melody filled the room and touched their cheeks like fingers, as if the hand that played moved among the congregation. They followed the music to see Lyn sitting at the foot of MaeAlice's coffin with an old guitar conjoined to her chest. Tears welled in Grace's eyes and spilled, unfettered.

Chapter 50: *Suku - Daniel St.John*

The ritual was over. Friends touched Nola with offers of condolence. Family members long forgotten listened to stories of the woman who could make anything grow.

"I know she loved being buried today," someone said. "It was her kind of weather. No way would she die in winter."

"Lord, no," someone agreed. "Had to be ninety-five today, and not a cloud in the sky."

A moment of silence followed other stories about her love for heat, and the repeated utterance, "God has her now."

Some had that look of wonder, trying to figure from where the money had come for her beautiful going home. It was impolite to ask, so they wandered through curious other groups, hoping someone would know.

The Estelle Samuda sat with Nola in the bedroom where MaeAlice had lived her last four years, and died. Neither sure what to say, each there for her own reason. Nola stared at the sweet potato perched with toothpicks; its vines draped across the dresser. "Needs water," she said.

Estelle Samuda watched her, feeling Nola's grief, knowing her relief; understanding Nola's guilt about the latter. "I'm glad you took care of her, Nola. In those early days of the stroke, she was ashamed to be here. We shared a lot over the years."

Nola listened to the woman who had known her mother for almost as long as she did. Estelle Samuda had known Nola's father too, longer than she knew MaeAlice. She was seventy-seven now; she'd live to be a hundred at the pace she was aging. The cane she used for more show than function rested in her lap and gave her hands something to do.

"She loved you. All of you. She didn't show it but that was the way she felt. To harm her children was like poking a bear. She'd killed to protect you." Estelle Samuda moved gently left and right, as if rocking to a song. The Nola listened. "I knew your daddy, too. Fine man. Good man. You favor him."

Nola hadn't heard mention of her father since she'd left New York, since her Aunt Sahra had said how much she resembled Daniel St.John.

"But it's Olivia the spitting image," Estelle Samuda added. "People think she got her mother's eyes, but no, that is Daniel St.John all over again. Even got his personality. Lord, she was a defiant child, had her own mind. Grew up more like her daddy than any one of you. Gave your mother a fit," she giggled.

"What happened to Daddy?" Nola asked. Perhaps it was the loss of her mother that made her ask about the man she barely knew. "Momma said he died but I never believed her."

"He did die, child."

"I know. It's just that I have dreams sometimes where I hear him calling my name. But there's always something wrong." Nola paused. "I know he's dead; I don't believe he just died, is what I mean. Ma'am, what happened to him?" This was the closest The Nola had come to confessing her attribute.

Estelle Samuda heard the voice of a child who needed to know why she had no father. She stiffened her rocking side to side. She remembered but could not tell this daughter that her father was dead, in part, because of her. That she helped The MaeAlice acquire a taste for vengeance.

The incident of Daniel's death was fresh, even now. The talks about Trinidad, their love for the island had brought them together. She was ten years younger than MaeAlice, full, fresh, desirable. Out of frustration, out of guilt, out of anger with himself, Daniel began to beat his wife. More than that, he was a proud man, a smart man, encumbered in the clutches of the south.

Olivia was six months old when The MaeAlice caught the two kissing: Daniel and Estelle. The kiss was harmless; consolation at a moment it felt like the right thing to do. But it never should have happened. The thought of hurting MaeAlice never crossed Estelle's mind. But she did. Daniel apologized for beating his wife, for cheating. He couldn't tell MaeAlice that the oppression of her North Carolina was a virus to his soul, his manhood. The same land that gave to her took from him. Daniel began to despise his wife's relationship with the land that fed him.

MaeAlice took it all, the beatings, the degradation; the sting of withheld affection. When he turned to Estelle, she could not take that. The MaeAlice put Daniel out of their home. He was gone two months before she took him back. He promised to be the husband she married. Little Daniel was born from that promise.

A year later things went very wrong. It was as if a thought that had been dismissed found its way home, not at all tired, but hungry.

The Estelle had gotten pictures and trinkets from home. She rushed to show Daniel and MaeAlice only to find them fighting. MaeAlice left in a fury. Little Daniel slept in a playpen; Olivia and Nola played nearby. Daniel calmed at seeing the gifts in her box. It was while in this mood, seeing him smile, feeling a twinge of what bound them that Estelle said, 'I miss this'.

The two sat quietly, watching the children, each holding a memory. Estelle Samuda waited for hours, expecting MaeAlice to return. Five o'clock came. She made dinner for the children, bathed them and put them to bed.

Daniel and Estelle finished the meal she'd prepared. MaeAlice had returned unnoticed. She stood in the kitchen, smelling honey and curry chicken, listening to them talk, hearing them laugh. Shortly, she heard her husband say, "I miss you, Estelle. I miss talking this way, I wish we could get back what we used to be."

"I wish we could, too, all of us," she replied. "But if you mean anything else, that was a mistake, Daniel. I love Mae like a sister; you know that. You're hurt right now, but you love your wife and you love those children. You're upset with her, that's all."

"I'm sick of her. All we do lately is fight. If I mention your name, she goes into a fit. Don't you see, she's jealous; she should be."

MaeAlice didn't hear any more words; instead, she felt what her husband did next. Sensed his hand move to the arm of this woman at her table. Without thinking, she picked up the knife Estelle Samuda had used to cut the chicken. Daniel did not see her but Estelle did. Before the woman could speak, MaeAlice brought the butcher's knife down across the hand whose fingers lay across Estelle's arm. The knife imbedded in the bone above Daniel's wrist. The hand that beat her, the hand that cheated. Blood splattered the table. MaeAlice walked away.

Estelle, eyes wide, mouth making some island noise, ran for a towel and wrapped his hand. By the time she got him to the hospital he'd passed out from loss of blood. Too

140

much alcohol. Too thin to clot. By the time the doctor saw him, when there were no more excuses to keep them waiting, he was ashen. They stitched his skin back together, bandaged him and sent him home.

It was two o'clock in the morning. Estelle decided not to wake MaeAlice. Instead she took him home with her. Over the next week, Daniel ran a fever. He'd lost too much blood. There was nothing to fight off infection, no strength to help him heal. In the second week since the incident, he died. MaeAlice had never gone to see Daniel but cried with everything within her when Estelle gave her the news. It was a vicious cut but she never thought he would die.

Estelle Samuda remembered Daniel St.John, and it saddened her. She decided there was nothing gained by telling this story. Besides, her culture did not permit speaking ill of the dead. Instead, she said to Nola, "Your father was a good man. The Lord called him home. Your mother loved him the best she knew how."

Chapter 51: *Love*

I sought out Olivia. She was not among any of the family groups listening to visitors talk. I found her at the old house on the yard swing, deep in thought. I chose not to pry. Perhaps it was reflection. Maybe it was the onset of grief. Maybe it was regret. In the days since Grandmother had died, neither of us spoke of our conversation that Sunday -- about mending the rift between mother and daughter. That wasn't my concern anymore. The last time Olivia had attended a funeral in Blessing was the day she'd put thirty-one years between us.

"So, what will you do now?" I asked, finally breaking my aunt's meditation.

A smile raised her cheekbones and partially closed her eyes. "Is that really what you want to ask me, Grace?" Olivia patted the seat beside her.

I sat in the spot she offered and looked off into the horizon, falling into the rhythm she had generated on the swing. "It's been nice having you back. I was just hoping you'd stay a while. But since the reason you came is over, I guess you'll be leaving again."

"I haven't decided. But I have to get back to my life eventually."

There was sweetness in Olivia's voice. We sat, gliding back and forth staring beyond the moment.

"It was interesting meeting Ms. York and Uncle Daniel's son. Did you know about him?" I asked.

"Denise came to DC shortly after I did. She was four months pregnant. Swore she wasn't coming back to North Carolina – not to Blessing anyway— but wanted someone in Daniel's family to know he was leaving a child behind."

"He looks a lot like him, doesn't he," I said. "Malice said his mom told him that Uncle Daniel died protecting grandmother."

"Malice is as handsome as his dad; almost like Daniel was reborn. Denise never married. She and Malice visited me some holidays. She sent me a card every year on Daniel's birthday. As Malice got older, we didn't see each other as often. Malice was away in academic camps."

"I can see that. He's really smart."

"I told Denise about Momma's condition and persuaded her to let Malice meet his grandmother before she died. She agreed to come, but then Shannon was shot. Still, she came the following week. "

I can only image the meeting between Grandmother and Malice. What was that like?"

"Denise went in first. She reminded Momma that she had come to Daniel's funeral. She told her that she and Daniel had dated and that and she had gotten pregnant. Denise apologized for not coming sooner and asked Momma to forgive her for keeping her grandchild a secret all these years.

"When Malice walked into the room, of course Momma couldn't see him that well. But as he got to her bed and sat down, she squinted, and called him Daniel. It was more like she was questioning her own eyes."

"I'm sure Grandma thought she was getting her son back."

"She asked Denise and me to leave the room. She wanted to talk to him alone. He was in there with the door closed for an hour."

"I'm just glad she got to see him; it had to make a difference. I remember how agitated she was the whole day before Uncle Daniel died. His death broke her. You and Slang brought home the pieces of what was left that night. So, I'm grateful to whatever gave her son back for even one hour."

Olivia and I intertwined our arms and stared out into the cemetery, each for different reasons. Silence moved us forward.

"Grace, I've had a strange feeling. I had it last night and again today before you came. In fact, I have it now."

Olivia hesitated. It wasn't because she was afraid to tell me; she knew I'd understand. The hesitation was involuntary.

"The day Momma died, we talked about making peace. I didn't get to do that."

"Let it go, Aunt Liv, it's not important anymore."

"I tried forgetting it, but all I heard in my head was, 'make peace'. When I called you for brunch, I had decided you were right. I knew you needed to resolve things with Nola, too, but before that could happen, you needed to know why she left you. So I told you, hoping it would help you put those years to rest. I never meant to hurt you."

I expected this conversation. I looked at the tree nearest Aunt Liv. "What would you have said?"

"I don't know..." Olivia thought for a minute and continued "...but each time I think about her, I get this feeling. It's not like missing her. It's not even grief. It's just there."

"When you think about her, what are you feeling?"

Olivia smiled. "You're good at this shrinking, I see."

"No changing the subject."

"It's weird. But I feel her holding me."

Olivia repositioned in the swing to look at me. "I was six years old, I think. We had gone to church one night for revival. Nola didn't go. She and Daniel stayed with Miss Samuda. Momma got a ride to church but when it let out, our ride was gone. You know how proud Momma was; she didn't ask for help and didn't ask for anything twice." Olivia chuckled. "First, she cursed the man's name on the church steps for leaving us, then we started walking. It was at least four miles to home. The road was pitch black. We could see a street lamp about a quarter mile up.

I made it past the first street light but knew I wouldn't make it to the next. Momma saw that. She knelt down and put my arms around her neck. She carried me on her back. For over three miles, I felt her hair in my face. It was as black as the highway and smelled like pomade. I've always liked that smell. I closed my eyes and felt the rise and fall of each step. I don't remember getting home. All I remember was waking up the next day and feeling different. It was the closest I'd ever felt to Momma. When I think about her now, I'm on her back, smelling her hair."

"Maybe Granny didn't need you to tell her anything. Maybe she's trying to tell you."

"Tell me what?"

"Of all the memories you could have when you think about her, you remember that one. And you get the same feeling now that you got then."

I touched Olivia's hand. I felt the millstone of a lifetime crumbling into dust, the tender beat of new life coming into being. I thought of my own mother— how Nola bore the burden of violence upon her spirit. I understood that the pieces of Nola's life wound themselves tightly around my own. It was no wonder she needed reassurance; from those compliments she took her worth. In them, she heard my father's love.

I understood the old man's words more deeply. Everything that happened to this tree happened to the others around it, even to the fruit it bore then and the fruit it would bear in the future. What had happened to Nola happened to me. I had grown apart from my mother, resented her in order to protect myself from the offense she endured.

Whatever had happened to Grandmother, however she became the person she was, mattered. Maybe her behavior was a dysfunction of birth. There was no way to know. Perhaps it didn't matter. Despite how people saw her, she accepted and endured.

Perhaps she didn't endure at all. Perhaps the weight of all the harm she had caused was too great. Her fights with the police contributed to her daughter's rape. The man she brought into her home killed her son. Her anger over the sickness she suffered while pregnant grew into resentment of her child. Then, one night, as if it would cleanse the guilt that grew out of her own hands, she took a life in retribution.

It could also be she lived in perfect alliance with God. Who was to say? Even the psychology I dispensed could not answer that question. As the old man had said, death is a mere step along the sacred journey. We meet it one way or another.

Grandmother loved. It broke the law to provide for her children, to raise them; took in grandchildren to help her daughter heal— a glimmer of penitence, a gesture of remorse. She became the hand that avenged her only son. All acts of love. But, in almost every way she tried, her love came out wrong. Twisted and tarnished. But it was love.

The swing continued its gentle motion, back and forth. Birds chirped in the trees nearby. A butterfly fought its way through the veil of heat.

I remembered my sojourn through the *Realm of Remembrance*, the place of regrets and roads not taken. Recalled the *Temple of Tears* where we cry for the things not said, the deeds not done; the harm we've caused or felt. Thoughts took me through the *Sanctuary of Service*, where we know love given and received, the mind of creation, the heartbeat of God.

I tried to recall a difference I'd made anywhere along the way. Nothing came. All the same, I was consoled knowing that in the *Sanctuary of Service*, we find unconditional acceptance despite what we might have been. Despite that we might have failed to do all that we could have done.

From that experience and the things I'd learned since, I resolved that family is not an act of birth; but the balm of love, the keeping of a promise made before birth. The holding of a hand while someone finds his way. I concluded that our journey through life is not to transcend our humanity but to embrace who we become because of it. To remember what we are, the thoughts of God. Gifts to each other. Creators of our homilies or curses.

Almost purposely, Olivia shifted on the swing and lifted her hand, ending my reflection. "What're you thinking?"

I sighed softly, giving myself time to process my thoughts. I wasn't sure I could put them into words. After a moment, I tried. "I'm thinking that we love the best we can, when we can, with the capacity we have, and what we know at that point in time. And at any given moment, for any given reason, we find ourselves loving that same thing, the same person, but from different eyes, a different heart. I know this sounds corny, but it's like... it's like..."

Seeing my difficulty, Olivia reached for my hand. Holding it tightly, she interrupted. "I know Grace... I know."

I turned to the tree again with a look of understanding. Grandmother looked at me with love that defied words. Olivia followed my stare. Though she saw nothing, the feeling she had described warmed her like the heat from Grandmother's stove. I felt it in her as surely as if there had been a shift in the Universe. Not knowing why, she smiled softly.

I smiled, too. "Yes. It's like that."

Chapter 52: *Return to Life*

Life was getting back to normal. Shannon and I took Wren for her checkup with Dr. Fugama. He announced she was progressing exceptionally. Mother and daughter had come through the ordeal of life after death with barely a scar.

After making an appointment for the next check up, Shannon and I arrived at a small café just before the end of lunch service. The place was nearly empty. We took a shaded table near the water. Wren slept in her carrier. I had decided now was as good a time as I'd get to share what I knew with Shannon.

"When you were in the hospital, Ted was there. While you were in surgery, I had a vision," I told her.

"What kind of vision?"

"I went to three places: The Realm of Remembrance, "The Temple of Tears--"

"Mom, what is this about?"

"It's about the decisions we make and the purpose we're given at birth."

"You sound like Ted."

"Sweetness, please listen. This is about that little girl right there."

Shannon relented.

"When Ted first arrived in Blessing, he tried to help Grandma by giving her money. I don't know if it was pride or some deep instinct, but she wouldn't take it. Before Grandma passed, Ted told me where he got the money. He also told me what he did with it. Were it not for the vision, I wouldn't be telling you this."

"Okay, you have my attention."

"Let me start at the beginning, in the Realm of Remembrance…"

148

Chapter 53: *The Birth of Q*

Shannon sat enrapt. "Fascinating story, Mom. I can see you had a profound experience. But I need you to connect the dots."

"In the Temple of Tears, I saw a pregnant woman who had been killed."

"You said the woman had a child that lived, a twin," Shannon added.

"Yes. The child was subjected to medical experiments." I waited a second before giving the punch line. "Dr. Fugama conducted those experiments." She continued eating her salad.

Apparently her time in laboratories had minimized any shock value in my comment. "The Voice said we are to build a research laboratory; that time is of the essence."

"I have to admit research is my dream, but what am I suppose to do in this lab?"

"I asked the Voice that, too? She said to follow your purpose."

"Which is what?"

"What do you think about doing when nobody is asking?"

Shannon smiled, "To tell you the truth, I want to explore genome technologies and their application to biological investigation."

"Is there a translation for that?"

Shannon laughed. "In simple English, I'm fascinated with understanding what allows us St. Johns to do what we do. Genetic sequencing is a huge part of that mystery. Did you know that women in a family all have the same genetic code in a particular sequence?"

The significance of that fact was profound for several reasons. "Wow. Then it sounds like the lab will be dedicated to Genomics," I replied.

"But clearly that is only part of the answer. What we are, and why, goes beyond science. We sacrifice our sons, for God-sake," Shannon added.

"Yes. According to Ted, in a time before time, we accepted transforming what it means to be human. But we are not the only ones to sacrifice a son."

That fact soaked in for the both of us. It was a Biblical tradition starting with God.

After a moment, Shannon added, "But I suspect this sacrificing of sons could have something to do with genetic selection. Genetics is a set of complex traits. Breeders have used hereditary selection for centuries to advance evolution in animals. Clearly family heredity and non-genetic factors, such as family, gender dominance and shared environmental effects are important. "

"Luckily, I get that," I said. "The family dynamics and our behaviors would be different with elder sons. But that doesn't explain the death of them all."

"Did you ask the Voice?"

"Girl, I just now learned about this genome effect. And the Voice didn't offer any information that didn't begin as a question from me."

"Maybe next time." Shannon said.

"Well, I do believe when you know the right question, you can get the right answer."

"So what do you think we're suppose to discover in this laboratory?"

"The Truth." I answered.

"The Truth? Which is what, exactly?"

"I don't know, yet. But Ted claims Wren is the answer. In fact, Wren is probably the question, too."

Shannon became more practical. "How do we spend three hundred thousand dollars without having to answer the obvious question?"

"We call Malice."

Chapter 54: *Everything Seeks Its Own*

Ten years passed. We celebrated Q-Labs' rise as a premiere medical facility in human genetics with a huge party. The milestone of its formation coincided with Wren's eleventh birthday. She surpassed us all intellectually and mystically.

Under Malice's influence, Shannon's expertise grew exponentially. She shadowed Malice on some of his projects. Sometimes what she learned put her on a totally unique track in her research.

Other times, she gave him a lead that made all the difference in his work. Their synchronicity was so strong the family heredity was clear. Malice was one of us. If his intellect and gift as a scientist were the result of Grandmother's sacrifice, then he had a higher purpose, too.

Malice and Shannon were a remarkable team but had to keep the family connection a secret. Malice's work was highly sensitive and he had concerns for our safety.

Other scientists studied their research on Neurological Indicators to Psychotic Pathology and Genetic Anomaly Correlations.

I supported their research as best I could, offering insight into the people they studied. Malice opened doors for us in some places and protected us from what was behind others. Dr. Fugama became a valued member of the brain pool.

Shannon never lost track of trying to break the code of the first-born effect. She studied our blood – us first-born women, and compared it to other immediate family members. Malice volunteered as the only son of a first-son of a first-born female. Since no first sons survived long enough to produce an offspring, he was our golden child.

Wren was gifted in ways that defied explanation. Like me, she was never sick, but also healed in a matter of hours from any wound. She helped her mother and Malice out of quagmires with clarity that left us all bewildered. She was only eleven. Her potential frightened us sometimes.

Needless to say, finding friends was a challenge for Wren. I knew how lonely she was for the connection to someone outside of family who understood her. One of the doors Malice opened was a school for advanced children. Even there, she was an anomaly, but happy. When I asked her about it, she said, "Well, Gaia, someone's going to be first. I'm okay that it's me."

Wren was equally fascinated with science, but her focus was plants, flowers in particular. What properties made some perennial and others die after a season. Why were some benign and others could kill. This, the persistent lethal properties of plants for seemingly no evolutionary reason, was the center of her study.

Wren had a botanical garden of some of these killer beauties: oleander, yellow jasmine, bloodroot, and Japanese yew, to name a few. She called the garden 'Beda' — short for beautiful death. I learned that the white willow tree on the edge of the cemetery that comforted me all those years ago actually had healing properties comparable to aspirin, but with longer lasting results. It shouldn't have survived in that environment, but Grandmother had planted it there.

Malice did not patronize Wren, but respected her as a scientist. A few months after the party, he came by with a file on a serial killer. When he was done, each first-born female looked at the other. Instantly, we knew. The killer was the child shown to me in the Temple of Tears.

This killer was the creation Ted had prophesied. He had been subjected to Dr. Fugama's experiments. The lab and the last ten years of research had to do with this young man. He was why Wren was born.

Both Shannon and I wondered if we were ready for this. Nothing she had developed or discovered could counteract what this young man had become.

We confronted Dr. Fugama. Wren had been given a variation of the formula injected into the serial killer. After all these years, he confessed the gender reassignment, but said Wren was unique. I already knew that, but listened to his story.

"Typically, boy babies could not absorb the material as successfully as girl babies. Never before had a boy transformed into a girl," he said. "Those who survived the procedure remained boys, but developed gender conflict. A small few eventually exhibited psychosis."

I retrieved another memory from the Temple of Tears. I had asked the Voice why God permits atrocities and suffering. It said, 'Everything God will do is already done; even our redemption. That is the Truth of God.' It said the rest is up to us. "Every person must find his or her own truth and do that, be that for which we are created. That is the balance of life."

153

I rejoined the conversation as Malice was adding more for our consideration.

"Those few also advanced genetically or physically beyond normalcy. They'd demonstrate what we typically call super human traits." He set a vile on the table containing a sample of something gooey, like a jellybean and a slide with a smear that looked like blood. "This man, this killer, is one of those. But he is beyond any and all scientific fact."

"Does he have a name?" I asked.

"The media dubbed him Mechisedec."

Shannon studied the contents on the slide under a microscope. The vile went into an analytic machine.

I continued the query with Malice and Dr. Fugama. "Let me guess; the people responsible have glimpsed this man's capabilities. They don't want the science he could provide or to know the mysteries he could unfold. That time has passed, right?"

Dr. Fugama, as the father of this creation, spoke first. "This young man is my legacy."

We heard the ambiguity and felt for him. He created a genius. And that genius was a threat to human existence. Dr. Fugama had had expectations of greatness in his field, and this creation was it. Regrettably, it could not be introduced to the world.

Shannon was transported to a place I'd never seen her go as she read the reports generated by her machines. Wren took the reports Malice provided. She learned the young man had been exposed to yellow jasmine in his mother's womb. So, she, too, became engrossed. They both took on a glow.

While they read their reports, I read Malice and Fugama. Their conflict was profound. Each fantasized this young man's power. Yet, they were afraid he was an uncontrollable genie. But who had summoned him and what wish was he granting? Ultimately, down to the layer of Truth, like their bosses, Malice and Fugama no longer wanted the science; they'd seen what he could do. What they had not yet seen, they feared. They'd put aside the curiosity of his evolution. His story would stay a mystery. They just wanted him dead.

EPILOGUE:

 C&

"I count my life and art as holy."

(from the Hippocratic Oath)

The Journey In

For those who are wondering about the conclusion of my travel into the realm of spirits, the experience is etched in my soul like the tablets given Moses.

When I leave the Temple of Tears, I am no longer walking. The water covers me like a bath until I no longer have form. I become a stream of water in the water's flow.

There must be a thousand specks of light. They look like fireflies. They blink and blend, making colors I've never seen. I'd always wished fireflies were in multi-color, so you can imagine my awe. The water changes colors, too, as if it and the lights are the same.

The colors emit a fine mist, like perfume spray. The smell is so wonderful I feel faint. In the distance I hear sounds— like tiny wind chimes.

I pass through the mist. The water that carried me here drains away. Every sensation of my body goes with it. I am aware that the blinks are reflecting my thoughts— like diamonds reflecting light. They are everywhere. Each blink makes me feel warm inside. It's the feeling I get from doing something nice for no reason. Like when I saw Shannon minutes after her birth. The first kiss I ever gave with my heart and got back. It feels like making love with love.

Suddenly, I understand. Every blinking color is goodness. They're acts of love. I feel beautiful, powerful. And yet, like a baby cuddled in its mother's arms. I don't want to leave.

But I hear the Voice in the distance. It says, "You have seen and heard. This place is forever. It is the *Sanctuary of Service*. All the good ever done through eternity is here.

The *Sanctuary of Service* is the source of Creation. That source is Love. Every soul begins here but not every soul returns. From love, we can create harm as well as good. But harm cannot enter here."

In the Sanctuary of Service, while talking with the Voice, my mind is more alert than I have ever been. Before me is a bowl of something like perfect pearls, soft like marshmellows. I know I am to eat them and welcome the sustenance." As I eat, I have the most enlightening conversation. I say to the Voice, "I thought the soul was only good?"

"There is truth in your assumption, but it is flawed. The word is a distortion of the original meaning. What you call a soul is really a 'cell'. But the process of living forms a layer of pollution on the cell. Much like the tarnish that forms on silver or brass. Underneath that dirt and grime, the silver is still silver and brass is still brass. In the *Temple of Tears*, a cell stays until it is washed of the tarnish acquired while living. The animal-like creatures you encountered were Wisdom and Compassion. They are the qualities every cell needs to make right decisions.

"How long a cell stays in the *Realm of Remembrance* or the *Temple of Tears* is up to it. Some choose to stay and punish themselves with regrets. Some hold onto the fear that ruled their lives. Others will not let go of the unworthy perceptions they've lived and believed about themselves. But each knows when it is ready. No one is forced; there is no timetable. Each cleanses and returns at its own pace. Love is timeless."

"Does that mean how well a soul behaves, whether it is good or bad while in the living world determines how fast it moves through The Temple of Tears?"

"There is no truth in that statement," the Voice answers. "Your question presumes that goodness is rewarded. That life has magic words. Goodness is not a token. There is no test, no graduation. The notion that you come back to learn lessons you missed comes from the same place as fairy tales. That assumption arose from humankind's fear of uncertainty and its desire for happy endings. Cells return in human form to help other cells. To be of service, to be a friend, a guide, a provider; a teacher, a companion; a creator of its own."

"What are we cells of?"

"Of that, which you call God."

"If we are cells of God, does that make us God?"

"A cell cannot contain all that is FEWA-SUKU-BEN-SWA. A cell is just that— a cell. Imagine that you are a brain. You know everything about your body, dictates how the body performs. As a brain, you send signals to the arms, feet, muscles, which have been coded to behave in certain ways based on the signal it receives. But, the brain can lose contact with the body through trauma or some other dysfunction, and yet, the rest of the organs continue to do what they were coded to do. The heart still beats, lungs still breathe."

I savor another pearl. "So, we are like organs which can function without God?"

The Voice replies, "Like the cells that make up the human body, we are the cells that make up FEWA-SUKU-BENSWA. Every cell is coded with knowledge of FEWA-SUKU-BENSWA, has a direct link to FEWA-SUKU-BEN-SWA but can function independently. The ability to function independently is what some call Free Will. While we are not FEWA-SUKU-BENSWA, we are *of* FEWA-SUKU-BENSWA. In the same way that you are not your mother,

160

but of her. You will always be linked to each other through a bond beyond birth, a bond that has no name. That bond which has no name is FEWA-SUKU-BENSWA, the Seen, the Unseen, the Known and the Unknown. Fire-Earth-Water-Air. Beneath; East North, South, West, Above.

I had heard that word before— first from the fire-talker. A light goes on in my head. 'SUKU!' Seen, Unseen, Known, Unknown!"

I could sense the Voice smile. It congratulates me with more Knowledge. "You are not born into a family to work out any issues from a past time. Sometimes cells come together and connect within the family, but more often the bond is outside that unit. When souls connect, they are cells from the same thought of God, they are predisposed to attract and bond with each other.

"Consider someone who has an attraction to a particular service or work—people who bond to art, or music, or science; who seem naturally good at something. That knowledge is in the cell. In the physical form cells may study to regain mastery, but the knowledge, the memory is there. All are healers."

The Voice said some like our clan of first-born women are healers of a different kind. That humans who know who they are and embrace that which is God in them— like musicians, scientists, inventors, athletes, and artists are more connected to the *Sanctuary* than those who do not embrace the talent given them. Some in the physical world call it 'gifted'. It is because they are more open to the energy of FEWA-SUKU-BENSWA. Their memories are less tarnished. A more accurate word is 'lifted'. Meaning that they've lifted a layer of the veil to the spiritual, the energy of their talent."

"Why isn't everyone?" I ask, and rest another pearl upon my tongue.

"Every person is gifted. That is, each is given knowledge specific to their purpose. You are sent forth to multiply, to expand your gifts. However, the transition from spirit into the living world is far more difficult, physically, than the transition back to spirit. The time span in the living world is short, relatively speaking, and many do not come into their memory or are able to work through their tarnish before they return to spirit. Some of you call these 'late bloomers'," she smiles.

In the physical form, all cells are Healers. When in the living world, your purpose is to help others to remember the Sanctuary, to help each other heal from the trauma of the transition. In human form, you are the cells of FE-WA-SUKU-BENSWA, sent to perform acts of FEWA-SU-KU-BENSWA. Some cells write, make music, some dance; bring laughter; some think. Some grow plants, some tend animals; some study the universe. All are healing acts. All are manifestations of FEWA-SUKU-BENSWA. All are meant to be co-creators with FEWA-SUKU-BENSWA."

"Then what are you," I asked.

"I am a Lagnawar. Simply, it means aware ascendant. Lagnawars provide information, like what you call intuition; we speak as your conscious. "

I asked the Voice to explain those people who hurt other people or take advantage? "Explain the liars, the thieves, the murderers. What kind of cells are they?"

"Birth is a very traumatic experience for a new thought. Imagine the trauma of being born into physical form from something you can't see or explain. Consider the difficulty you have bringing an idea into existence. It is not an easy manifestation.

"Sometimes cells are affected in ways that distort their connection to FEWA-SUKU-BENSWA. Therefore, the capacity to care for another is corrupted. Those affected this way may have less mercy and kindness, a deformation of God's intent. Even the ones who make it through successfully are affected but in lesser degrees. With the right support, at the right time, a soul can be healed — cleansed of the tarnish, so to speak, while in the human existence.

"That's what you and Shannon do. It's what friends do for one another. It's why monks pray."

The Voice paused to give me time to absorb the message. "There is also a group with virtually no memory of the Sanctuary, or their purpose. Some foolishly think they can 'fix' those people. Fixers think if they love enough, sympathize, and show enough patience, they can redeem what they call a lost soul. A cell that has truly corrupted its humanity will not find it in the face or the hand of anyone but God. The best thing one can do when confronted with such a cell is to let it pass, let it find its own way. Civilization has adopted ways to remove these people from society.

"Likewise, you have the lotus eaters."

"Lotus eaters?"

"Yes, those who live their lives in blank apathy. They do nothing, they care for nothing outside their own basic needs."

"Do you mean those who do alcohol and drugs in excess?"

"Yes, they are included as lotus eaters. But those who indulge in excess are but a few in comparison. Most lotus eaters simply exist and call it God's will that they do nothing. They squander their gifts through indifference. Some

163

lotus eaters addict themselves to things; like their careers, possessions, and appearance."

I've known a few like that," I said. "It's as if they've been exposed somehow to the feelings I got from the blinking lights."

"Exactly. But they have lost the connection to FEWA-SUKU-BENSWA because they obsess in self-indulgence."

"I see."

"Lastly, the greatest reason some don't connect is Fear. One of the most devastating emotions humans have taught each other is to doubt themselves and mistrust each other. Society even fears some who are lifted because they don't understand them.

"Through fear, some deny their greatness. They are not attuned to FEWA-SUKU-BENSWA because they are taught that punishment is the consequence of every action. So they seek to punish themselves, or others, first."

"Then, what is evil," I asked. "Does the Devil exist?"

"There is no Being called the Devil. But the Universe is created in duality, so it is a logical notion to think that there is an opposite of what is called God. Only religion makes that claim. People who fear need something or someone to blame for their decisions. FEWA-SUKU-BEN-SWA has no nemesis, no opposite. And since FEWA-SU-KU-BENSWA is everything, what would be the point?"

"But there is evil in the world, right, People do sin."

"What you know as evil is a loss of compassion. As dual beings, such a person is out of balance. The polar opposite of Good has come to mean a Bad thing. It is simply a variation of energy. It, too, has purpose— to help balance. Imagine your life if every thought, every action came forth perfectly formed and executed? Upon what would you judge that thought or action?

"Imagine this: what if the people labeled evil are serving their purpose? What if their actions allow you to judge your own? What if those individuals are the polish for your growth and enlightenment? Would you thank them?

"And sin... well, in simplest terms, it means an interruption in the signal, the signal being the connection to the source of Love. Your mathematicians use the phrase accurately when they talk about waves and frequencies and so forth."

I immediately understand. Sig – sin: sin is a malfunction in the signal! The "g," the God connection is malfunctioning! Each of us operates on varying, unique vibrations. Through that vibration we experience God. And for all kinds of reasons, the vibration, the signal, can be interrupted.

The Voice continued. "Remember, the Sanctuary of Service is a place of perfection, a place of profound knowledge. The other realms are necessary to purge the soul of the impurities it acquires during transition and while in the human experience to restore the connection. Some fear the transition because the cell knows it must pass through the Temple of Tears. Those who fear don't want to see and feel their malfeasance upon FEWA-SUKU-BENSWA."

"Yeah, I guess that could be hell," I smirked.

"Exactly," the Voice said. "Some call it that."

How many transitions are there?" I asked.

"A revered cell long ago, said it best. He said, 'in my Father's house are many mansions.'"

"Did you just say..."

"No. FEWA-SUKU-BENSWA has no likeness. FEWA-SUKU-BENSWA was given the male personality during a time when one form of energy thought itself more favored than another. The gender division started because cells

165

who came as male feared the perceived power that the cells who came as female had over them. In fact, male and female are a single thought from which all races sprang, just like the multitude of birds and creatures of the sea sprang from single thoughts. But fear has caused some to seek control rather than be equal partners in the care of all that came through creation."

I breathe deeply; all the pearls are gone, but, oddly, I feel lighter. Suddenly I realize I have been transitioning through a realm since the first question I asked.

The Voice smiles, "Yes. You have passed through the *Navel of Ma'at*, the place of all truth, wisdom, balance, and order."

The knowledge helps me remember why I am here. I tell the Voice that I must get to the Mothers.

The Voice ignores my concern. "Soon. You have one more realm on your journey," she says. "It is an eminent place. A Sacred Place. Even as you arrive at your destination, it is only the beginning."

"What is it?"

"Some call it 'The Pearly Gate'. We call it the *Road to Resurrection*."

~o~

This is the story I shared with Shannon. I didn't know it then, but my journey also held the answer to our date with Mechesidec.

CʒCʒ

I would rather have a mind opened by wonder than one closed by belief. ~ *Gerry Spence*

m.e.b.smith is the author of *The Scent of Gardenia: A Killing in Princeville, The Keepers of Carifa,* and the upcoming*: What I Know About God.* Her stories intertwine, each having a thread in the other, because as she says, "All things are connected."

Thank you for the gift of your time.

This story attempts to answer questions I had as a child about life and death, good, evil; right and wrong; love and loss, and all that is in between. At its core, *Blood of Their Sons* is about relationships, about decisions we make. It's about the transformations we undergo because of those decisions.

What I've concluded is this:

We love and do the best we can at that point in time. Who, among us, may judge that for anyone else?

Readers' Comments

◁▲

I feel as though I've just read something holy...
J D Miller

It's a book you can talk about and pull from end-
lessly; there's something on every page.
W McNair

I came away with a message to live life, and not
judge how you live it as right or wrong...
D Holeman

WOW..what a story!.
withheld